Praise for Samuel R. Delany's Other Books

"Nevèrÿon series is a major and unclassifiable achievement in contemporary American literature." **—Fredric R. Jameson**

"Delany's work exists on a kind of borderline—between theory and literary practice, between canonical and popular culture, between academic and nonacademic culture—a borderline familiar to feminist theory and cultural critique. The Nevèrÿon series is one of the most sustained meditations we have on the complex intersections of sexuality, race, and subjectivity in contemporary cultures." **—Constance Penley**

"[Delany] works real magic in these pages . . . Portions of 'Atlantis: Model 1924' linger, even loom, in my memory, and I suspect they will long endure there."

—Hungry Mind Review

"'Atlantis: Model 1924' is neither SF nor fantasy . . . [but it] has an odd, unsettling power not usually associated with mainstream fiction . . . should be of interest to all Delany fans for its wondrous (and entirely characteristic) ability to introduce us to a living world. It's a talent very close to time travel —or magic." *—Locus*

"One of the most interesting pieces now published, ['The Tale of Plagues and Carnivals'] is a melding of fiction, commentary and diary, bringing together Delany's Nevèrÿon characters with people from the equally fantastical setting of modern New York during the early years of the AIDS epidemic . . . redolent of Defoe's 'The Plague Years,' [it] is a moving and powerful statement that strikes home." *—San Francisco Chronicle*

"This may be the most successfully experimental work yet from an author for whom language and story are inseparable . . . ['The Tale of Plagues and Carnivals' is] a lengthy masterpiece, whose kaleidoscopic fragments cross the border between fact and fiction, extracting one from the other with meticulous precision."   —*Library Journal*

"A Joycean tour de force of a novel [*Dhalgren*] seems to me . . . to stake a better claim than anything else in this country in the last quarter-century . . . to a permanent place as one of the enduring monuments of our national literature."
        —Jeff Riggenbach, *Libertarian Review*

"The very best ever to come out of the science fiction field . . . The usefulness of *Dhalgren* to you and to me is beyond question. Having experienced it, you will stand taller, understand more, and press your horizons back a little further away than you ever knew they would go . . . a literary landmark."
        —Theodore Sturgeon, *Galaxy Bookshelf*

"[*Trouble on Triton*] is classic Delany that maintains a cutting edge of sheer platinum. Delany sets his interrogation of the myth and politics of a central culture within an infinitely richer galaxy of interwoven margins. The dazzle always illuminates: the novel offers vision-altering thrills on the order of paradigm shifts or sex at its most rapturously cataclysmic."
        —Earl Jackson, Jr., author of *Fantastic Living: The Speculative Autobiographies of Samuel R. Delany*

The Einstein Intersection

Other Books by the Author

Fiction

The Jewels of Aptor
The Fall of the Towers:
   Out of the Dead City
   The Towers of Toron
   City of a Thousand Suns
The Ballad of Beta-2
Babel-17
Empire Star
Nova
Driftglass (stories)
Equinox (The Tides of Lust)
Dhalgren
Trouble on Triton (Triton)
Distant Stars (stories)
Stars in My Pockets Like Grains of Sand
Return to Nevèrÿon:
   Tales of Nevèrÿon
   Neveryóna
   Flight from Nevèrÿon
   Return to Nevèrÿon (The Bridge of Lost Desire)
Driftglass/Starshards (collected stories)
They Fly at Çiron
The Mad Man
Hogg
Atlantis: Three Tales

Nonfiction

The Jewel-Hinged Jaw
The American Shore
Heavenly Breakfast
Starboard Wine
The Motion of Light in Water
Wagner/Artaud
The Straits of Messina
Silent Interviews
Longer Views: Extended Essays

Samuel R. Delany

The Einstein Intersection

FOREWORD BY NEIL GAIMAN

Wesleyan University Press
PUBLISHED BY UNIVERSITY PRESS OF NEW ENGLAND
HANOVER AND LONDON

Wesleyan University Press

Published by University Press of New England, Hanover, NH 03755

Copyright © 1967 by Samuel R. Delany

Printed in the United States of America

5 4 3 2 1

CIP data appear at the end of the book

First published by Ace Books in 1967. Subsequently reprinted by Bantam Books.
Wesleyan University Press paperback 1998.

For Don Wollheim,
a responsible man in all meanings
to and for what is within,
and Jack Gaughan,
for what is without.

Foreword

BY NEIL GAIMAN

Two misconceptions are widely held about written science fiction.

The initial misconception is that SF (at the time Delany wrote *The Einstein Intersection* many editors and writers were arguing that Speculative Fiction might be a better use of the initials, but that battle was lost a long time back) is about the future, that it is, fundamentally, predictive. Thus *1984* is read as Orwell's attempt to predict the world of 1984, as Heinlein's *Revolt in 2100* is seen as an attempted prediction of life in 2100. But those who point to the rise of any version of Big Brother, or the many current incarnations of the Anti-Sex League, or the mushrooming power of Christian fundamentalism as evidence that Heinlein or Orwell was engaged in forecasting Things To Come are missing the point.

The second misconception, a kind of second-stage misconception, easy to make once one has traveled past the "SF is about predicting the future" conceit, is this: SF is about the vanished present. Specifically SF is solely about the time when it was written. Thus, Alfred Bester's *Demolished Man* and *Tiger! Tiger!* (better known in the United States as *The Stars My Destination*) are about the 1950s, just as William Gibson's *Neuromancer* is about the 1984 we lived through in reality. Now this is true, as far as it goes, but is no more true for SF than for any other practice of writing: our tales are always the fruit of our times. SF, as with all other art, is the product of its era, reflecting or reacting against or illuminating the prejudices, fears, and assumptions of the period in which it was written. But there is more to SF than this: one does not only read Bester to decode and reconstruct the 1950s.

What is important in good SF, and what makes SF that lasts, is how it talks to us of our present. What does it tell us *now?* And, even more important, what will it always tell us? For the point where SF becomes a rich and significant practice of writing is the point where it is about something bigger and more important than Zeitgeist, whether the author intended it to be or not.

The Einstein Intersection (a pulp title imposed on this book from without—Delany's original title for it was *A Fabulous, Formless Darkness*) is a novel that is set in a time after the people like us have left the Earth and *others* have moved into our world, like squatters into a furnished house, wearing our lives and myths and dreams uncomfortably but conscientiously. As the novel progresses, Delany weaves myth, consciously and un-self-consciously: Lobey, our narrator, is Orpheus, or plays Orpheus, as other members of the cast will find themselves playing Jesus and Judas, Jean Harlow (out of Candy Darling) and Billy the Kid. They inhabit our legends awkwardly: they do not fit them.

The late Kathy Acker has discussed Orpheus at length, and Samuel R. Delany's role as an Orphic prophet, in her introduction to the Wesleyan Press edition of *Trouble on Triton*. All that she said there is true, and I commend it to the reader. Delany is an Orphic bard, and *The Einstein Intersection,* as will become immediately apparent, is Orphic Fiction.

In the oldest versions we have of the story of Orpheus it appears to have been simply a myth of the seasons: Orpheus went into the Underworld to find his Euridice, and he brought her safely out into the light of the sun again. But we lost the happy ending a long time ago. Delany's Lobey, however, is not simply Orpheus.

The Einstein Intersection is a brilliant book, self-consciously suspicious of its own brilliance, framing its chapters with quotes from authors ranging from Sade to Yeats (are these the owners of the house into which the squatters have moved?) and with extracts from the author's own notebooks kept while writing the book and wandering the Greek Islands. It was written by a young author in the milieu he has described in *The Motion of Light in Water* and *Heavenly Breakfast*, his two autobiographical works, and here he is writing about music and love, growing up, and the value of stories as only a young man can.

One can see this book as a portrait of a generation that dreamed that new drugs and free sex would bring about a fresh dawn and the rise of *homo superior*, wandering the world of the generation before them like magical children walking through an abandoned city—through the ruins of Rome, or Athens, or New York: that the book is inhabiting and reinterpreting the myths of the people who came to be known as the hippies. But if that were all the book was, it would be a poor sort of tale, with little resonance for now. Instead, it continues to resonate.

So, having established what *The Einstein Intersection* is not, what is it?

I see it as an examination of myths, and of why we need them, and why we tell them, and what they do to us, whether we understand them or not. Each generation replaces the one that came before. Each generation newly discovers the tales and truths that came before, threshes them, discovering for itself what is wheat and what is chaff, never knowing or caring or even understanding that the generation who will come after them will discover that some of their new timeless truths were little more than the vagaries of fashion.

The Einstein Intersection is a young man's book, in every way: it is the book of a young author, and it is the story of a young man going into the big city, learning a few home truths about love, growing up, and deciding to go home (somewhat in the manner of Fritz Leiber's protagonist from *Gonna Roll the Bones*, who takes the long way home, around the world).

These were the things that I learned from the book the first time I read it, as a child: I learned that writing could, in and of itself, be beautiful. I learned that sometimes what you do not understand, what remains beyond your grasp in a book, is as magical as what you can take from it. I learned that we have the right, or the obligation, to tell old stories in our own ways, because they are our stories, and they must be told.

These were the things I learned from the book when I read it again, in my late teens: I learned that my favorite SF author was black, and understood now who the various characters were based upon, and, from the extracts from the author's notebooks, I learned that fiction was mutable—there was something dangerous and exciting about the idea that a black-haired character would gain red hair and pale skin in a second draft (I also learned there could be second drafts). I discovered that the idea of a book and the book itself were two different things. I also enjoyed and appreciated how much the author doesn't tell you: it's in the place that readers bring themselves to the book that the magic occurs.

I had by then begun to see *The Einstein Intersection* in context as part of Delany's body of work. It would be followed by *Nova* and *Dhalgren*, each book a quantum leap in tone and ambition beyond its predecessor, each an examination of mythic structures and the nature of writing. In *The Einstein Intersection* we encounter ideas that could break cover as SF in a way they were only beginning to do in the real world, particularly in the portrait of the nature of sex and sexuality that the book draws for us: we are given, very literally, a third, transitional sex, just as we are given a culture ambivalently obsessed with generation.

Rereading the book recently as an adult I found it still as beautiful, still as strange; I discovered passages—particularly toward the twisty end—that had once been opaque were now quite clear. Truth to tell, I now found Lo Lobey an unconvincing heterosexual: while the book is certainly a love story, I found myself reading it as the story of Lobey's courtship by

Kid Death, and wondering about Lobey's relationships with various other members of the cast. He is an honest narrator, reliable to a point, but he has been to the city after all, and it has left its mark on the narrative. And I found myself grateful, once again, for the brilliance of Delany and the narrative urge that drove him to write. It is good SF, and even if, as some have maintained (including, particularly, Samuel R. Delany), literary values and SF values are not necessarily the same, and the criteria—the entire critical apparatus—we use to judge them are different, this is still fine literature, for it is the skilled writing of dreams, and of stories, and of myths. That it is good SF, whatever that is, is beyond question. That it is a beautiful book, uncannily written, prefiguring much fiction that followed, and too long neglected, will be apparent to the readers who are coming to it freshly with this new edition.

I remember, as a teen, encountering Brian Aldiss's remark on the fiction of Samuel R. Delany in his original critical history of SF, *Billion Year Spree*: quoting C. S. Lewis, Aldiss commented that Delany's telling of how odd things affected odd people was an oddity too much. And that puzzled me, then and now, because I found, and still find, nothing odd or strange about Delany's characters. They are fundamentally human; or, more to the point, they are, fundamentally, us.

And that is what fiction is for.

October 1997

The Einstein Intersection

It darkles, (tinct, tint) all this our funanimal world.

James Joyce, *Finnegans Wake*

I do not say, however, that every delusion or wandering
of the mind should be called madness.

Erasmus of Rotterdam, *The Praise of Folly*

There is a hollow, holey cylinder running from hilt to point
in my machete. When I blow across the mouthpiece in the
handle, I make music with my blade. When all the holes are
covered, the sound is sad—as rough as rough can be and be
called smooth. When all the holes are open, the sound pipes
about, bringing to the eye flakes of sun on water, crushed
metal. There are twenty holes. And since I've been playing
music I've been called all different kinds of fool—more times
than Lobey, which is my name.

What I look like?

Ugly and grinning most of the time. That's a whole lot of
big nose and gray eyes and wide mouth crammed on a small
brown face proper for a fox. That, all scratched around with
spun brass for hair. I hack most of it off every two months or
so with my machete. Grows back fast. Which is odd, because
I'm twenty-three and no beard yet. I have a figure like a bowl-
ing pin, thighs, calves, and feet of a man (gorilla?) twice my
size (which is about five-nine) and hips to match. There was a
rash of hermaphrodites the year I was born, which doctors
thought I might be. Somehow I doubt it.

Like I say, ugly. My feet have toes almost as long as my fingers, and the big ones are semi-opposable. But don't knock it: once I saved Little Jon's life.

We were climbing the Beryl Face, slipping around on all that glassy rock, when Little Jon lost his footing and was dangling by one hand. I was hanging by *my* hands, but I stuck my foot down, grabbed him up by the wrist, and pulled him back where he could step on something.

At this point Lo Hawk folds his arms over his leather shirt, nods sagely so that his beard bobs on his ropy neck, says: "And just what were you two young Lo men doing on Beryl Face in the first place? It's dangerous, and we avoid danger, you know. The birthrate is going down, down all the time. We can't afford to lose our productive youth in foolishness." Of course it isn't going down. That's just Lo Hawk. What he means is that the number of *total norms* is going down. But there's plenty of births. Lo Hawk is from the generation where the number of non-functionals, idiots, mongoloids, and cretins was well over fifty percent. (We hadn't adjusted to your images yet. Ah, well.) But now there are noticeably more functionals than non-functionals; so no great concern.

Anyway, not only do I bite my fingernails disgracefully, I also bite my toenails.

And at this point I recall sitting at the entrance of the source-cave where the stream comes from the darkness and makes a sickle of light into the trees, and a blood spider big as my fist suns himself on the rock beside me, belly pulsing out from the sides of him, leaves flicking each other above. Then La Carol walks by with a sling of fruit over her shoulder and the kid under her arm (we had an argument once whether it was mine or not. One day it had my eyes, my nose, my ears. The next, "Can't you see it's Lo Easy's boy? Look how strong he is!" Then we both fell in love with other people and now we're friends again) and she makes a face and says, "Lo Lobey, what *are* you doing?"

"Biting my toenails. What does it look like?"

"Oh, really!" and she shakes her head and goes into the woods towards the village.

But right now I prefer to sit on the flat rock, sleep, think, gnaw, or sharpen my machete. It's my privilege, so La Dire tells me.

Until a little while ago, Lo Little Jon, Lo Easy, and Lo me herded goats together (which is what we were doing on the Beryl Face: looking for pasture). We made quite a trio. Little Jon, though a year older than me, will till death look like a small black fourteen-year-old with skin smooth as volcanic glass. He sweats through his palms, the soles of his feet, and his tongue. (No real sweat glands: piddles like a diabetic on the first day of winter, or a very nervous dog.) He's got silver mesh for hair—not white, silver. The pigment's based on the metal pure; the black skin comes from a protein formed around the oxide. None of that rusty iron brown of melanin that suntans you and me. He sings, being a little simple, running and jumping around the rocks and goats, flashing from head and groin and armpits, then stops to cock his leg (like a nervous dog, yeah) against a tree-trunk, glancing around with embarrassed black eyes. Smiling, those eyes fling as much light, on a different frequency, as his glittering head. He's got claws—hard, sharp horny ones, where I have nubs. He's not a good Lo to have mad at you.

Easy, on the other hand, is large (about eight feet tall), furry (umber hair curls all down the small of his back, makes ringlets on his belly), strong (that three hundred and twenty-six pounds of Easy is really a lot of rock jammed jagged into his pelt: his muscles have corners), and gentle. Once I got angry at him when one of the fertile nannies fell down a rock chimney.

I saw it coming. The ewe was the big blind one who had been giving us perfect norm triplets for eight years. I stood on one foot and threw rocks and sticks with the other three limbs. It takes a rock on the head to get Easy's attention; he was much closer than I was.

"Watch it, you non-functional, lost-Lo mongoloid! She's gonna fall in the—" At which point she did.

Easy stopped looking at me with his what-are-you-throwing-stones-at-me-for? face, saw her scrabbling at the edge, dove for her, missed, and both of them started bleating. I put my all behind the rock that caught him on the hip and almost cried. Easy did.

He crouched at the chimney edge, tears wetting the fur on his cheeks. The ewe had broken her neck at the chimney's bottom. Easy looked up and said, "Don't hurt me no more, Lobey. That"—he knuckled his blue eyes, then pointed down—"hurts too much already." What can you do with a Lo like that? Easy has claws too. All he ever uses them for is to climb the titan palms and tear down mangoes for the children.

Generally we did a good job with the goats, though. Once Little Jon leaped from the branch of an oak to the back of a lion and tore out its throat before it got to the herd (and rose from the carcass, shook himself, and went behind a rock, glancing over his shoulder). And as gentle as he is, Easy crushed a blackbear's head with a log. And I got my machete, all ambidextrous, left footed, right handed, or vice versa. Yeah, we did a good job.

Not no more.

What happened was Friza.

"Friza" or "La Friza" was always a point of debate with the older folk-doctors and the elders who have to pass on titles. She looked normal: slim, brown, full mouth, wide nose, brass-colored eyes. I think she may have been born with six fingers on one hand, but the odd one was non-functional, so a travelling doctor amputated it. Her hair was tight, springy, and black. She kept it short, though once she found some red cord and wove it through. That day she wore bracelets and copper beads, strings and strings. She was beautiful.

And silent. When she was a baby, she was put in the kage with the other non-functionals because she didn't move. No La. Then a keeper discovered she didn't move because she already knew how; she was agile as a squirrel's shadow. She was taken out of the kage. Got back her La. But she never spoke. So at age eight, when it was obvious that the beautiful orphan was mute, away went her La. They couldn't very well put her back in the kage. Functional she was, making baskets, plowing, an expert huntress with the bolas. That's when there was all the debate.

Lo Hawk upheld: "In my day, La and Lo were reserved for total norms. We've been very lax, giving this title of purity to any functional who happens to have the misfortune to be born in these confusing times."

To which La Dire replied: "Times change, and it has been an unspoken precedent for thirty years that La and Lo be bestowed on any functional creature born in this our new home. The question is merely how far to extend the definition of functionality. Is the ability to communicate verbally its *sine qua non?* She is intelligent and she learns quickly and thoroughly. I move for *La Friza.*"

The girl sat and played with white pebbles by the fire while they discussed her social standing.

"The beginning of the end, the beginning of the end," muttered Lo Hawk. "We must preserve something."

"The end of the beginning," sighed La Dire. "Everything must change." Which had been their standing exchange as long as I remember.

Once, before I was born, so goes the story, Lo Hawk grew disgruntled with village life and left. Rumors came back: he'd gone to a moon of Jupiter to dig out some metal that wormed in blue veins through the rock. Later: he'd left the Jovian satellite to sail a steaming sea on some world where three suns cast his shadows on the doffing deck of a ship bigger than our whole village. Still later: he was reported chopping away through a substance that melted to poisonous fumes someplace so far there were no stars at all during the year-long nights. When he had been away seven years, La Dire apparently decided it was time he came back. She left the village and returned a week later—with Lo Hawk. They say he hadn't changed much, so nobody asked him about where he'd been. But from his return dated the quiet argument that joined La Dire and Lo Hawk faster than love.

". . . must preserve," Lo Hawk.

". . . must change," La Dire.

Usually Lo Hawk gave in, for La Dire was a woman of wide reading, great culture, and wit; Lo Hawk had been a fine hunter in his youth and a fine warrior when there was need. And he was wise enough to admit in action, if not words, that such need had gone. But this time Lo Hawk was adamant:

"Communication is vital, if we are ever to become human beings. I would sooner allow some short-faced dog who comes from the hills and can approximate forty of fifty of our words to make known his wishes, than a mute child. Oh, the battles my youth has seen! When we fought off the giant spiders, or when the wave of fungus swept from the jungle, or when we destroyed with lime and salt the twenty-foot slugs that pushed up from the ground, we won these battles because we could speak to one another, shout instructions, bellow a warning, whisper plans in the twilit darkness of the source-caves. Yes, I would sooner give La or Lo to a talking dog!"

Somebody made a nasty comment: "Well, you couldn't very well give her a Le!" People snickered. But the older folk are very good at ignoring that sort of irreverence. Everybody ignores a Le anyway. Anyway, the business never did get settled. Towards moondown people wandered off, when somebody suggested adjournment. Everyone creaked and groaned to his feet. Friza, dark and beautiful, was still playing with the pebbles.

Friza didn't move when a baby because she knew how already. Watching her in the flicker (I was only eight myself) I got the first hint why she didn't talk: she picked up one of the pebbles and hurled it, viciously, at the head of the guy who'd made the remark about "Le." Even at eight she was sensitive. She missed, and I alone saw. But I saw too the snarl that twisted her face, the effort in her shoulders, the way her toes curled—she was sitting crosslegged—as she threw it. Both fists were knotted in her lap. You see, she didn't use her hands or feet. The pebble just rose from the dirt, shot through the air, missed its target, and chattered away through low leaves. But I saw: she *threw* it.

Each night for a week I have lingered on the wild flags of the waterfront, palaces crowding to the left, brittle light crackling over the harbor in the warm autumn. TEI goes strangely. Tonight when I turned back into the great trapezoid of the Piazza, fog hid the tops of the red flagpoles. I sat on the base of one nearest the tower and made notes on Lobey's hungers. Later I left the decaying gold and indigo of the Basilica and wandered through the back alleys of the city till well after midnight. Once I stopped on a bridge to watch the small canal drift through the close walls beneath the nightlamps and clotheslines. At a sudden shrieking I whirled: half a dozen wailing cats hurled themselves about my feet and fled after a brown rat. Chills snarled the nerves along my vertebrae. I looked back at the water: six flowers—roses—floated from beneath the bridge, crawling over the oil. I watched them till a motorboat puttering on some larger waterway nearby sent water slapping the foundations. I made my way over the small bridges to the Grand Canal and caught the Vaporetto back to Ferovia. It turned windy as we floated beneath the black wood arch of the Ponte Academia; I was trying to assimilate the flowers, the vicious animals, with Lobey's adventure—each applies, but as yet I don't quite know how. Orion straddled the water. Lights from the shore shook in the canal as we passed beneath the dripping stones of the Rialto.

Writer's Journal, Venice, October 1965

In a few lines I shall establish how Maldoror was virtuous during his first years, virtuous and happy. Later he became aware he was born evil. Strange fatality!

Isidore Ducasse (Comte de Lautreamont),
The Songs of Maldoror

All prologue to why Lo Easy, Lo Little John, and Lo me don't herd goats no more.

Friza started tagging along, dark and ambiguous, running and jumping with Little Jon in a double dance to his single song and my music, play-wrestling with Easy, and walking with me up the brambly meadow holding my hand—whoever heard of La-ing or Lo-ing somebody you're herding goats with, or laughing with, or making love with. All of which I did with Friza. She would turn on a rock to stare at me with leaves shaking beside her face. Or come tearing towards me through the stones; between her graceful gait and her shadow in the rocks all suspended and real motion was. And was released when she was in my arms laughing—the one sound she did make, loving it in her mouth.

She brought me beautiful things. And kept the dangerous away. I think she did it the same way she threw the pebble. One day I noticed that ugly and harmful things just weren't happening: no lions, no condor bats. The goats stayed together; the kids didn't get lost and kept from cliffs.

"Little Jon, you don't have to come up this morning."

"Well, Lobey, if you don't think—"

"Go on, stay home."

So Easy, Friza, and me went out with the goats.

The beautiful things were like the flock of albino hawks that moved to the meadow. Or the mother woodchuck who brought her babies for us to see.

"Easy, there isn't enough work for all of us here. Why don't you find something else to do?"

"But I like coming up here, Lobey."

"Friza and me can take care of the herd."

"But I don't mi—"

"Get lost, Easy."

He said something else and I picked up a stone in my foot and hefted it. He looked confused, then lumbered away. Imagine, coming on like that with Easy.

Friza and I had the field and the herd to ourselves alone. It stayed good and beautiful with unremembered flowers beyond rises when we ran. If there were poisonous snakes, they turned off in lengths of scarlet, never coiling. And, ah! did I make music.

Something killed her.

She was hiding under a grove of lazy willows, the trees that droop lower than weeping, and I was searching and calling and grinning—she shrieked. That's the only sound I ever heard her make other than laughter. The goats began to bleat.

I found her under the tree, face in the dirt.

As the goats bleated, the meadow went to pieces on their rasping noise. I was silent, confused, amazed by my despair.

I carried her back to the village. I remember La Dire's face as I walked into the village square with the limber body in my arms.

"Lobey, what in the world . . . How did she . . . Oh, *no!* Lobey, no!"

So Easy and Little Jon took the herd again. I went and sat at the entrance to the source-cave, sharpened my blade, gnawed my nails, slept and thought alone on the flat rock. Which is where we began.

Once Easy came to talk to me.

"Hey, Lobey, help us with the goats. The lions are back. Not a lot of them, but we could still use you." He squatted, still towering me by a foot, shook his head. "Poor Lobey." He ran his hairy fingers over my neck. "We need you. You need us. Help us hunt for the two missing kids?"

"Go away."

"Poor Lobey." But he went.

Later Little Jon came. He stood around for a minute thinking of something to say. But by the time he did, he had to go behind a bush, got embarrassed, and didn't come back.

Lo Hawk came too. "Come hunting, Lo Lobey. There's a bull been seen a mile south. Horns as long as your arm, they say."

"I feel rather non-functional today," I said. Which is not the sort of thing to joke about with Lo Hawk. He retired, humphing. But I just wasn't up to his archaic manner.

When La Dire came, though, it was different. As I said, she has great wit and learning. She came and sat with a book on the other side of the flat rock, and ignored me for an hour. Till I got mad. "What are you doing here?" I asked at last.

"Probably the same thing you are."

"What's that?"

She looked serious. "Why don't you tell me?"

I went back to my knife. "Sharpening my machete."

"I'm sharpening my mind," she said. "There is something to be done that will require an edge on both."

"Huh?"

"Is that an inarticulate way of asking what it is?"

"Huh?" I said again. "Yeah. What is it?"

"To kill whatever killed Friza." She closed her book. "Will you help?"

I leaned forward, feet and hands knotting, opened my mouth—then La Dire wavered behind tears. I cried. After all that time it surprised me. I put my forehead on the rock and bawled.

"Lo Lobey," she said, the way Lo Hawk had, only it was different. Then she stroked my hair, like Easy. Only different. As I gained control again I sensed both her compassion and embarrassment. Like Little Jon's; different.

I lay on my side, feet and hands clutching each other, sobbing towards the cavity of me. La Dire rubbed my shoulder, my bunched, distended hip, opening me with gentleness and words:

"Let's talk about mythology, Lobey. Or let's you listen. We've had quite a time assuming the rationale of this world.

The irrational presents just as much of a problem. You remember the legend of the Beatles? You remember the Beatle Ringo left his love Maureen even though she treated him tender. He was the one Beatle who did not sing, so the earliest forms of the legend go. After a hard day's night he and the rest of the Beatles were torn apart by screaming girls, and he and the other Beatles returned, finally at one, with the great rock and the great roll." I put my head in La Dire's lap. She went on. "Well, that myth is a version of a much older story that is not so well known. There are no 45's or 33's from the time of this older story. There are only a few written versions, and reading is rapidly losing its interest for the young. In the older story Ringo was called Orpheus. He too was torn apart by screaming girls. But the details are different. He lost his love—in this version Eurydice—and she went straight to the great rock and the great roll, where Orpheus had to go to get her back. He went singing, for in this version Orpheus was the greatest singer, instead of the silent one. In myths things always turn into their opposites as one version supersedes the next."

I said, "How could he go into the great rock and the great roll? That's all death and all life."

"He did."

"Did he bring her back?"

"No."

I looked from La Dire's old face and turned my head in her lap to the trees. "He lied, then. He didn't really go. He probably went off into the woods for a while and just made up some story when he came back."

"Perhaps," La Dire said.

I looked up again. "He wanted her back," I said. "I know he wanted her back. But if he had gone any place where there was even a chance of getting her, he wouldn't have come back unless she was with him. That's how I know he must have been lying. About going to the great rock and the great roll, I mean."

"All life is a rhythm," she said as I sat up. "All death is a rhythm suspended, a syncopation before life resumes." She picked up my machete. "Play something." She held the handle out. "Make music."

I put the blade to my mouth, rolled over on my back, curled around the bright, dangerous length, and licked the sounds. I didn't want to but it formed in the hollow of my tongue, and breathing carried it into the knife.

Low; first slow; I closed my eyes, feeling each note in the quadrangle of shoulder blades and buttocks pressed on the rock. Notes came with only the meter of my own breathing, and from beneath that, there was the quickening of the muscles of my fingers and toes that began to cramp for the faster, closer dance of the heart's time. The mourning hymn began to quake.

"Lobey, when you were a boy, you used to beat the rock with your feet, making a rhythm, a dance, a drum. Drum, Lobey!"

I let the melody speed, then flailed it up an octave so I could handle it. That means only fingers.

"Drum, Lobey!"

I rocked to my feet and began to slap my soles against the stone.

"Drum!"

I opened my eyes long enough to see the blood spider scurry. The music laughed. Pound and pound, trill and warble, and La Dire laughed for me too, to play, hunched down while sweat quivered on my nape, threw up my head and it dribbled into the small of my back, while I, immobile above the waist, flung my hips, beating cross rhythms with toes and heels, blade up to prick the sun, new sweat trickling behind my ears, rolling the crevices of my corded neck.

"Drum, my Lo Ringo; play, my Lo Orpheus," La Dire cried. "Oh, Lobey!" She clapped and clapped.

Then, when the only sound was my own breath, the leaves, and the stream, she nodded, smiling. "Now you've mourned properly."

I looked down. My chest glistened, my stomach wrinkled

and smoothed and wrinkled. Dust on the tops of my feet had become tan mud.

"Now you're almost ready to do what must be done. Go now, hunt, herd goats, play more. Soon Le Dorik will come for you."

All sound from me stopped. Breath and heart too, I think, a syncopation before the rhythm resumed. "Le Dorik?"

"Go. Enjoy yourself before you begin your journey."

Frightened, I shook my head, turned, fled from the cave mouth.

Le—

Suddenly the wandering little beast fled, leaving in my
lap—O horror—a monster and misshapen maggot with
a human head.
　"Where is your soul that I may ride it!"
　　　　　　　Aloysius Bertrand, "The Dwarf"

Come ALIVE! You're in the PEPSI generation!
　　　　　　　Current catchphrase (*Commercial*)

　—Dorik.

An hour later I was crouching, hidden, by the kage. But
the kage-keeper, Le Dorik, wasn't around. A white thing (I
remember when the woman who was Easy's mother flung it
from her womb before dying) had crawled to the electrified
fence to slobber. It would probably die soon. Out of sight I
heard Griga's laughter; he had been Lo Griga till he was sixteen. But something—nobody knew if it was genetic or not—
rotted his mind inside his head, and laughter began to gush
from his gums and lips. He lost his Lo and was placed in the
kage. Le Dorik was probably inside now, putting out food,
doctoring where doctoring would do some good, killing
when there was some person beyond doctoring. So much
sadness and horror penned up there; it was hard to remember they were people. They bore no title of purity, but they
were people. Even Lo Hawk would get as offended over a
joke about the kaged ones as he would about some titled citi-
zen. "You don't *know* what they did to them when I was a boy,
young Lo man. You never saw them dragged back from the
jungle when a few did manage to survive. You didn't see the

barbaric way complete norms acted, their reason shattered bloody by fear. Many people we call Lo and La today would not have been allowed to live had they been born fifty years ago. Be glad *you* are a child of more civilized times." Yes, they were people. But this is not the first time I had wondered what it feels like to keep such people—Le Dorik?

I went back to the village.

Lo Hawk looked up from re-thonging his cross-bow. He'd piled the power cartridges on the ground in front of the door to check the caps. "How you be, Lo Lobey?"

I picked a cartridge out with my foot, turned it over. "Catch that bull yet?"

"No."

I pried the clip back with the tip of my machete. It was good. "Let's go," I said.

"Check the rest first."

While I did, he finished stringing the bow, went in and got a second one for me; then we went down to the river.

Silt stained the water yellow. The current was high and fast, bending ferns and long grass down, combing them from the shore like hair. We kept to the soggy bank for about two miles.

"What killed Friza?" I asked at last.

Lo Hawk squatted to examine a scarred log: tusk marks. "You were there. You saw. La Dire only guesses."

We turned from the river. Brambles scratched against Lo Hawk's leggings. I don't need leggings. My skin is tough and tight. Neither does Easy or Little Jon.

"I didn't see anything," I said. "What does she guess?"

An albino hawk burst from a tree and gyred away. Friza hadn't needed leggings either.

"Something killed Friza that was non-functional, something about her that was non-functional."

"Friza was functional," I said. "She was!"

"Keep your voice down, boy."

"She kept the herd together," I said more softly. "She could make the animals do what she wanted. She could move the dangerous things away and bring the beautiful ones nearer."

"Bosh," said Lo Hawk, stepping over ooze.

"Without a gesture or a word, she could move the animals anywhere she wanted, or I wanted."

"That's La Dire's nonsense you've been listening to."

"No. I saw it. She could move the animals just like the pebble."

Lo Hawk started to say something else. Then I saw his thoughts backtrack. "What pebble?"

"The pebble she picked up and threw."

"*What* pebble, Lobey?"

So I told him the story. "And it was functional," I concluded. "She kept the herd safe, didn't she? She could have kept it even without me."

"Only she couldn't keep herself alive," Lo Hawk said. He started walking again.

We kept silent through the whispering growth, while I mulled. Then:

"*Yaaaaaa*—" on three different tones.

The leaves whipped back and the Bloi triplets scooted out. One of them leaped at me and I had an armful of hysterical, redheaded ten-year-old.

"*Hey* there now," I said sagely.

"Lo Hawk, Lobey! Back there—"

"Watch it, will you?" I added, avoiding an elbow.

"—back there! It was stamping, and pawing the rocks—" This from one of them at my hip.

"Back where?" Lo Hawk asked. "What happened?"

"Back there by the—"

"—by the old house near the place where the cave roof falls in—"

"—the bull came up and—"

"—and he was awful big and he stepped—"

"—he stepped on the old house that—"

"—we was playing inside—"

"Hold up," I said and put 3-Bloi down. "Now where was all this?"

They turned together and pointed through the woods.

Hawk swung down his crossbow. "That's fine," he said. "You boys get back up to the village."

"Say—" I caught 2-Bloi's shoulder. "Just how big was he?" Inarticulate blinking now.

"Never mind," I said. "Just get going."

They looked at me, at Lo Hawk, at the woods. Then they got.

In silent consensus we turned from the river through the break in the leaves from which the children had tumbled.

A board, shattered at one end, lay on the path just before us as we reached the clearing. We stopped over it, stepped out between the sumac branches.

And there were a lot of other smashed boards scattered across the ground.

A five-foot section of the foundation had been kicked in, and only one of the four supporting beams was upright.

Thatch bits were shucked over the yard. A long time ago Carol had planted a few more flowers in this garden, when, wanting to get away from the it-all of the village, we had moved down here to the old thatched house that used to be so cozy, that used to be . . . she had planted the hedge with the fuzzy orange blooms. You know that kind?

I stopped by one cloven print where petals and leaves had been ground in a dark mandala on the mud. My feet fit inside the print easily. A couple of trees had been uprooted. A couple more had been broken off above my head.

It was easy to see which way he had come into the clearing. Bushes, vines, and leaves had erupted inward. Where he had left, everything sort of sagged out.

Lo Hawk ambled into the clearing swinging his crossbow nonchalantly.

"You're not really that nonchalant, are you?" I asked. I looked around again at the signs of destruction. "It must be huge."

Lo Hawk threw me a glance full of quartz and gristle. "You've been hunting with me before."

"True. It can't have been gone very long if it just scared the kids away," I added.

Hawk stalked towards the place where things were sagging. I hurried after.

Ten steps into the woods, we heard seven trees crash somewhere: three—pause—then four more.

"Of course, if he's that big he can probably move pretty far pretty fast," I said.

Another three trees.

Then a roar:

An unmusical sound with much that was metallic in it, neither rage nor pathos, but noise, heaved from lungs bigger than smelting bellows, a long sound, then echoing while the leaves turned up beneath a breeze.

Under green and silver we started again through the cool, dangerous glades.

And step and breathe and step.

Then in the trees to our left—

He came leaping, and that leap rained us with shadow and twigs and bits of leaf.

Turning his haunch with one foreleg over here and a hindleg *way* the hell over there, he looked down at us with an eye bloodshot, brown, and thickly oystered in the corners. His eyeball must have been big as my head.

The wet, black nostrils steamed.

He was very noble.

Then he tossed his head, breaking branches, and hunkered with his fists punched into the ground—they were hands with horny hairy fingers thick as my arm where he should have had forehooves—bellowed, reared, and sprang away.

Hawk fired his crossbow. The shaft flapped like a darning needle between the timbers of his flank. He was crashing off.

The bark of the tree I'd slammed against chewed on my back as I came away.

"Come on," Hawk hollered, as he ran in the general direction the man-handed bull had.

And I followed that crazy old man, running to kill the beast. We clambered through a cleft of broken rock (it hadn't been broken the last time I'd come wandering down here through the trees—an afternoon full of sun spots and breezes and Friza's hand in mine, on my shoulder, on my cheek). I jumped down onto a stretch of moss-tongued brick that paved the forest here and there. We ran forward and—

Some things are so small you don't notice them. Others are so big you run right into them before you know what they are. It was a hole, in the earth and the side of the mountain, that we almost stumbled into. It was a ragged cave entrance some twenty meters across. I didn't even know it was there till all that sound came out of it.

The bull suddenly roared from the opening in the rock and trees and brick, defining the shape of it with his roaring.

When the echo died, we crept to the crumbled lip and looked over. Below I saw glints of sunlight on hide, turning and turning in the pit. Then he reared, shaking his eyes, his hairy fists.

Hawk jerked back, even though the claws on the brick wall were still fifteen feet below us.

"Doesn't this tunnel go into the source-cave?" I whispered. Before something that grand, one whispers.

Lo Hawk nodded. "Some of the tunnels, they say, are a hundred feet high. Some are ten. This is one of the bigger arterioles."

"Can it get out again?" Stupid question.

On the other side of the hole the horned head, the shoulders emerged. The cave-in had been sloped there. He had climbed out. Now he looked at us, crouched there. He bellowed once with a length of tongue like foamy, red canvas.

Then he leaped at us across the hole.

He didn't make it, but we scurried backward. He caught the lip with the fingers of one hand—I saw black gorges break about those nails—and one arm. The arm slapped around over the earth, searching for a hand-hold.

From behind me I heard Hawk shout (I run faster than he does). I turned to see that hand rise from over him!

He was all crumpled up on the ground. The hand slapped

a few more times (*Boom—Boom! Boom!*) and then arm and fingers slipped, pulling a lot of stone and bushes and three small trees, down, down, down.

Lo Hawk wasn't dead. (The next day they discovered he had cracked a rib, but that wasn't till later.) He began to curl up. I thought of an injured bug. I thought of a sick, sick child.

I caught him up by the shoulders just as he started to breathe again. "Hawk! Are you—"

He couldn't hear me because of the roaring from the pit. But he pulled himself up, blinking. Blood began trickling from his nose. The beast had been slapping with cupped palm. Lo Hawk had thrown himself down, and luckily most of the important parts of him, like his head, had suffered more from air-blast than concussion.

"Let's get out of here!" and I began to drag him towards the trees.

When we got there, he was shaking his head.

"—no, wait, Lobey—" came over in his hoarse voice during a lull in the roaring.

As I got him propped against a trunk, he grabbed my wrist.

"Hurry, Hawk! Can you walk? We've got to get away. Look, I'll carry you—"

"No!" The breath that had been knocked out of him lurched back.

"Oh, come *on,* Hawk! Fun is fun. But you're hurt, and that thing is a lot bigger than either of us figured on. It must have mutated from the radiation in the lower levels of the cave."

He tugged my wrist again. "We have to stay. We have to kill it."

"Do you think it will come up and harm the village? It hasn't gone too far from the cave yet."

"That—" He coughed. "That has nothing to do with it. I'm a hunter, Lobey."

"Now, look—"

"And I have to teach you to hunt." He tried to sit away from the trunk. "Only it looks like you'll have to learn this lesson by yourself."

"Huh?"

"La Dire says you have to get ready for your journey."

"Oh, for goodness—" Then I squinted at him, all the crags and age and assurance and pain in that face. "What I gotta do?"

The bull's roar thundered up from the caved-in roof of the source-cave.

"Go down there; hunt the beast—and kill it."

"No!"

"It's for Friza."

"How?" I demanded.

He shrugged. "La Dire knows. You must learn to hunt, and hunt well." Then he repeated that.

"I'm all for testing my manhood and that sort of thing. But—"

"It's a different reason from that, Lobey."

"But—"

"Lobey." His voice nestled down low and firm in his throat. "I'm older than you, and I know more about this whole business than you do. Take your sword and crossbow and go down into the cave, Lobey. Go on."

I sat there and thought a whole lot of things. Such as: bravery is a very stupid thing. And how surprised I was that so much fear and respect for Lo Hawk had held from my childhood. Also, how many petty things can accompany pith, moment, and enterprise—like fear, confusion, and plain annoyance.

The beast roared again. I pushed the crossbow farther up my arm and settled my machete handle at my hip.

If you're going to do something stupid—and we all do—it might as well be a brave and foolish thing.

I clapped Lo Hawk's shoulder and started for the pit.

On this side the break was sharp and the drop deep. I went around to the sagging side, where there were natural ledges of root, earth, and masonry. I circled the chasm and scrambled down.

Sun struck the wall across from me, glistening with moss. I

dropped my hand from the moist rock and stepped across an oily rivulet whose rainbow went out under my shadow. Somewhere up the tunnel, hooves clattered on stone.

I started forward. There were many cracks in the high ceiling, here and there lighting on the floor a branch clawing crisped leaves or the rim of a hole that might go down a few inches, a few feet, or drop to the lowest levels of the source-cave that were thousands of feet below.

I came to a fork, started beneath the vault to the left, and ten feet into the darkness tripped and rolled down a flight of shallow steps, once through a puddle (my hand splatting out in the darkness), once over dry leaves (they roared their own roar beneath my side), and landed at the bottom in a shaft of light, knees and palms on gravel.

Clatter!

Clatter!

Much closer: *Clatter!*

I sprang to my feet and away from the telltale light. Motes cycloned in the slanting illumination where I had been. And the motes stilled.

My stomach felt like a loose bag of water sloshing around on top of my gut. Walking towards that sound—he was quiet now and waiting—was no longer a matter of walking in a direction. Rather: pick that foot up, lean forward, put it down. Good. Now, pick up the other one, lean forward—

A hundred yards ahead I suddenly saw another light because something very large suddenly filled it up. Then it emptied.

Clack! Clack! Clack!

Snort!

And three steps could carry him such a long way.

Then a lot of *clacks!*

I threw myself against the wall, pushing my face into dirt and roots.

But the sound was going off.

I swallowed all the bitter things that had risen into my throat and stepped back from the wall.

The Einstein Intersection o 23

With a quick walk that became a slow run I followed him under the crumbling vaults.

His sound came from the right.

So I turned right and into a sloping tunnel so low that ahead of me I heard his horns rasp on the ceiling. Stone and scale and old lichen chittered down at his hulking shoulders, then to the ground.

The gutter on the side of the tunnel had coated the stone with fluorescent slime. The trickle became a stream as the slope increased till the frothing light raced me on the left.

Once his hooves must have crossed a metal floor-plate, because for a half-dozen steps orange sparks glittered where he stepped, lighting him to the waist.

He was only thirty meters ahead of me.

Sparks again as he turned a corner.

I felt stone under the soles of my feet, then cold, smooth metal. I passed some leaves, blown here by what wind, that his hooves had ignited. They writhed with worms of fire, glowing about my toes. And for moments the darkness filled with autumn.

I reached the corner, started around—

Facing me, he bellowed.

His foot struck a meter from my foot, and from this close the sparks lit his raw eyes, his polished nostrils.

His hand came between his eyes and me, falling! I rolled backward, grabbing for my machete.

His palm—flat this time, Hawk—clanged on the metal plate where I had been. Then it fell again toward where I was.

I lay on my back with the hilt of the blade on the floor, point up. Very few people, or bulls, can hit a ten-penny nail and drive it to the hilt. Fortunately.

He jerked me from the floor, pinioned to his palm, and I got flung around (holding on to the blade with hands and feet and screaming) an awful lot.

He was screaming too, butting the ceiling and lots of things falling. From twenty feet he flung me loose. The blade pulled free, my flute filled with his blood, and I hurled into the wall and rolled down.

His right shoulder struck the right wall. He lurched. His left shoulder struck the left wall. And his shadow flickering on the dripping ceiling was huge.

He came down towards me, as I dragged my knees over a lot of wrought stone beneath me, rocked back to my feet (something was sprained too), and tried to look at him, while he kept going out between steps.

Beside me in the wall was a grating about three feet high, with the bars set askew. It was probably a drain. I fell through. And dropped about four feet to a sloping floor.

It was pitch-black above me and there was a hand grasping and grasping in the dark. I could hear it scrabbling against the wall. I took a swipe overhead, and my blade struck something moving.

Roaaaaaa . . . !

The sound was blunted behind stone. But from my side came the sharp retort of his palm as he started slapping.

I dived forward. The slope increased, and suddenly I slid down a long way, very fast, getting even more scraped up. I came up sharply against pipes.

Eyes closed, I lay there, the tip of the crossbow uncomfortable under my shoulder, the blade handle biting between the bars and my hip. Then the places that were uncomfortable got numb.

If you really relax with your eyes closed, the lids pull slowly open. When I finally relaxed, light filled my eyes from the bottoms up like milk poured in bowls.

Light?

I blinked.

Gray light beyond the grating, the gray that sunlight gets when it comes from around many corners. Only I was at least another two levels down. I lay behind the entrance to another drain like the one I'd leaped through.

Then somewhere, the roar of a bull, echoing through these deep stones.

I pulled myself up on the bars, elbows smarting, shoulders bruised, and something pulled sore in the bulk of my thigh. I gazed into the room below.

At one time there was a floor level with the bottom of this grating, but most of it had fallen in a long and longer time ago. Now the room was double height and the grate was at least fifteen feet above the present floor.

Seventy, eighty meters across, the room was round. The walls were dressed stone, or bare rock, and rose in gray slabs towards the far light. There were many vaulted entrances into dark tunnels.

In the center was a machine.

While I watched, it began to hum wistfully to itself, and several banks of lights glittered into a pattern, froze, glittered into another. It was a computer from the old time (when you owned this Earth, you wraiths and memories), a few of which still chuckled and chattered throughout the source-cave. I'd had them described to me, but this was the first I'd seen.

What had wakened me—

(and had I been asleep? And had I dreamed, remembering now with the throbbing image clinging to the back of my eyes, Friza?)

—was the wail of the beast.

Head down, hide bristling over the hunks of his shoulders, gemmed with water from the ceiling, he hunched into the room, dragging the knuckles of one hand, the other—the one I had wounded twice—hugged to his belly.

And on three legs, a four legged animal (even one with hands) limps.

He blinked about the room, and wailed again, his voice leaving pathos quickly and striking against rage. He stopped the sound with a sniff, then looked around and knew that I was there.

And I wanted very much not to be.

I squatted now behind the grating and looked back and up and down and couldn't see any way out. Hunt, Lo Hawk had said.

The hunter can be a pretty pathetic creature.

He swung his head again, tasting the air for me, his injured hand twitching high on his belly.

(The hunted's not so hot either.)

The computer whistled a few notes of one of the ancient tunes, some chorus from *Carmen*. The bull-beast glanced at it uncomprehending.

How was I to hunt him?

I brought the crossbow down and aimed through the grate. It wouldn't mean anything unless I got him in the eye. And he wasn't looking in the right direction.

I lowered the bow and took up my blade. I brought it to my mouth and blew. Blood bubbled from the holes. Then the note blasted and went reeling through the room.

He raised his head and stared at me.

Up went the bow; I aimed through the bars, pulled the trigger—

Raging forward with horns shaking, he got bigger and bigger and bigger through the frame of stone. I fell back while the roar covered me, closing my eyes against the sight: his eye gushed about my shaft. He grasped the bars behind which I crouched.

Metal grated on stone, stone pulled from stone. And then the frame was a lot bigger than it had been. He hurled the crumpled grate across the room to smash into the wall and send pieces of stone rolling.

Then he reached in and grabbed me, legs and waist, in his fist, and I was being waved high in the air over his bellowing face (left side blind and bloody) and the room arching under me and my head flung from shoulder to shoulder and trying to point the crossbow down—one shaft broke on the stone by his hoof a long way below. Another struck awfully close to the shaft that Lo Hawk had shot into his side. Waiting for a wall of stone to come up and jelly my head, I fumbled another arrow into the slot.

His cheek was sheeted with blood. And suddenly there was more blood. The shaft struck and totally disappeared in the blind well of bone and lymph. I saw the other eye cloud as though someone had overblown the lens with powdered lime.

He dropped me.

Didn't throw me; just dropped. I grabbed the hair on his wrist. It slipped through my hands, and I slid down his forearms to the crook of his elbow.

Then his arm began to fall. Slowly I turned upside down. The back of his hand hit the floor, and his hind feet were clacking around on the stone.

He snorted, and I began to slide back down his forearm towards his hand, slowing myself by clutching at the bristles with feet and hands. I rolled clear of his palm and staggered away from him.

The thing in my thigh that was sprained throbbed.

I stepped backward and couldn't step any more.

He swayed over me, shook his head, splattering me with his ruined eye. And he was grand. And he was *still* strong, dying above me. And he was huge. Furious, I swayed with him in my fury, my fists clutched against my hips, tongue stifled in my mouth.

He was great and he was handsome and he *still* stood there defying me while dying, scoffing at my bruises. Damn you, beast who would be greater than—

One arm buckled, a hindleg now, and he collapsed away from me, crashing.

Something in the fistsful of darkness that were his nostrils thundered and roared—but softer, and softer. His ribs rose to furrow his side, fell to rise again; I took up the bow and limped to the bloody tears of his lips, fitted one final shaft. It followed the other two into his brain.

His hands jerked three feet, then fell *(Boom! Boom!)* relaxing now.

When he was still, I went and sat on the base of the computer and leaned against the metal casing. Somewhere inside it was clicking.

I hurt. Lots.

Breathing was no fun any more. And I had, somewhere during all this, bitten the inside of my cheek. And when I do that, it gets me so mad I could cry.

I closed my eyes.

"That was very impressive," someone said close to my right ear. "I would love to see you work with a *muleta*. Olé! Olé! First the *verónica*, then the *paso doble!*"

I opened my eyes.

"Not that I didn't enjoy your less sophisticated art."

I turned my head. There was a small speaker by my left ear. The computer went on soothingly:

"But you are a dreadfully unsophisticated lot. All of you. Young, but *très charmant*. Well, you've fought through this far. Is there anything you'd like to ask me?"

"Yeah," I said. Then I breathed for a while. "How do I get out of here?" There were a lot of archways in the wall, a lot of choices.

"That is a problem. Let me see." The lights flickered over my lap, the backs of my hands. "Now, of course, had we met before you entered, I could have waved out a piece of computer tape and you would have taken the end and I would have unwound it after you as you made your way into the heart to face your fate. But instead, you have arrived here and found me waiting. What do you desire, hero?"

"I want to go home," I said.

The computer went *tsk-tsk-tsk.* "Other than that."

"You really want to know?"

"I'm nodding sympathetically," it said.

"I want Friza. But she's dead."

"Who was Friza?"

I thought. I tried to say something. With the exhaustion, all that came was a catch in my throat that might have sounded like a sob.

"Oh." After a moment, gently: "You've come into the wrong maze, you know."

"I have? Then what are you doing here?"

"I was set here a long time ago by people who never

dreamed that you would come. Psychic Harmony and Entangled Deranged Response Associations, that was my department. And you've come down here hunting through my memories for your lost girl."

Yes, I may have just been talking to myself. I was very tired.

"How do you like it up there?" PHAEDRA asked.

"Where?"

"Up there on the surface. I can remember back when there were humans. They made me. Then they all went away, leaving us alone down here. And now you've come to take their place. It must be rather difficult, walking through their hills, their jungles, battling the mutated shadows of their flora and fauna, haunted by their million-year-old fantasies."

"We try," I said.

"You're basically not equipped for it," PHAEDRA went on. "But I suppose you have to exhaust the old mazes before you can move into the new ones. It's hard."

"If it means fighting off those—" I jutted my chin towards the carcass on the stone. "Yeah, it is."

"Well, it's been fun. I miss the *revueltas,* the maidens leaping over the horns and spinning in the air to land on the sweating back, then vaulting to the sands! Mankind had style, baby! You may get it yet, but right now your charm is a very young thing."

"Where did they go, PHAEDRA?"

"Where your Friza went, I suppose." Something musical was happening behind my head within the metal. "But you aren't human and you don't appreciate their rules. You shouldn't try. Down here we try to follow what you're doing for a few generations, and questions get answered we would never have even thought of asking. On the other hand, we sit waiting out centuries for what would seem like the most obvious and basic bits of information about you, like who you are, where you're from, and what you're doing here. Has it occurred to you that you might get her back?"

"Friza?" I sat up. "Where? How?" La Dire's cryptic statements came back.

"You're in the wrong maze," PHAEDRA repeated. "And I'm the wrong girl to get you into the right one. Kid Death along for a little while and maybe you can get around him enough to put your foot in the door, finger in the pie, your two cents in, as it were."

I leaned forward on my knees. "PHAEDRA, you baffle me."

"Scoot," PHAEDRA said.

"Which way?"

"Again. You've asked the wrong girl. Wish I could help. But I don't know. But you'd better get started. When the sun goes down and the tide goes out, this place gets dark, and the gillies and ghosties gather 'round, shouting."

I heaved to my feet and looked at the various doorways. Maybe a little logic? The bull-beast had come from the doorway over there. So that's the one I went in.

The long, long dark echoed with my breath and falling water. I tripped over the first stairway. Got up and started climbing. Bruised my shoulder on the landing, groped around and finally realized I had gotten off into a much smaller passage that didn't *seem* like it was going anywhere.

I took up my machete and blew out the last of the blood. The tune now winding with me lay notes over the stone like mica flakes that would do till light came.

Stubbed my toe.

Hopped, cursed, then started walking again alone with the lonely, lovely sounds.

"Hey—"

"—Lobey, is—"

"—is that you?" Young voices came from behind stone.

"Yes! Of course it's me!" I turned to the wall and put my hands against the rock.

"We snuck back—"

"—to watch, and Lo Hawk—"

"—he told us to go down into the cave and find you—"

"—cause he thought you might be lost."

I pushed my machete back into my scabbard. "Fine. Because I am."

"Where are you?"

"Right here on the other side of this—" I was feeling around the stones again, above my head this time. My fingers came on an opening. It was nearly three feet wide. "Hold on!" I hoisted myself up, clambered onto the rim, and saw faint light at the end of a four-foot tunnel. I had to crawl through because there wasn't room to stand.

At the other end I stuck my head out and looked down at the upturned faces of the Bloi triplets. They were standing in a patch of light from the roof.

2-Bloi rubbed his nose with the back of his fist and sniffed.

"Oh," 1-Bloi said. "You were up there."

"More or less." I jumped down beside them.

"Damn!" 3-Bloi said. "What happened to you?" I was speckled with bull's eye, scratched, bruised, and limping.

"Come on," I said. "Which way is out?"

We were only around the corner from the great cave-in. We joined Lo Hawk on the surface.

He stood (remember, he had a cracked rib that nobody was going to find out about till the next day) against a tree with his arms folded. He raised his eyebrows to ask me the question he was waiting with.

"Yeah," I said. "I killed it. Big deal." I was sort of tired.

Lo Hawk shooed the kids ahead of us back to the village. As we tromped through the long weeds, suddenly we heard stems crash down among themselves.

I almost sat down right there.

It was only a boar. His ear could have brushed my elbow. That's all.

"Come on." Lo Hawk grinned, raising his crossbow.

We didn't say anything else until after we had caught and killed the pig. Lo Hawk's powered shaft stunned it, but I had to hack it nearly in half before it would admit it was dead. After *el toro?* Easy. Bloody to the shoulders, we trudged back finally, through the thorns, the hot evening.

The head of the boar weighed fifty pounds. Lo Hawk lugged it on his back. We'd cut off all four hams, knotted them together, and I carried two on each shoulder, which was another two hundred and seventy pounds. The only way we could have gotten the whole thing back was to have had Easy along. We'd nearly reached the village when he said, "La Dire noticed that business with Friza and the animals. She's seen other things about you and others in the village."

"Huh? Me?" I asked. "What about me?"

"About you, Friza, and Dorik the kage-keeper."

"But that's silly." I'd been walking behind him. Now I drew abreast. He glanced across the tusk. "You were all born the same year."

"But we're all—different."

Lo Hawk squinted ahead, then looked down. Then he looked at the river. He didn't look at me.

"I can't do anything like the animals or the pebble."

"You can do other things. Le Dorik can do still others."

He still wasn't looking at me. The sun was lowering behind copper crested hills. The river was brown. He was silent. As clouds ran the sky, I dropped behind again, placed the meat beside me, and fell on my knees to wash in the silted water.

Back at the village I told Carol if she'd dress the hams she could have half my share. "Sure," but she was dawdling over a bird's nest she'd found. "In a minute."

"And hurry up, huh?"

"All right. All right. Where are you in such a rush to?"

"Look, I will polish the tusks for you and make a spearhead for the kid or something if you will *just keep off my back!*"

"Well, I—look, it's not your kid anyway. It's—"

But I was sprinting towards the trees. I guess I must have still been upset. My legs sprint pretty fast.

It was dark when I reached the kage. There was no sound from behind the fence. Once something blundered against the wire, whined. Sparks and a quick shadow. I don't know which side it came from. No movement from Le Dorik's shack. Maybe Dorik was staying inside the kage on same project. Sometimes they mated in there, even gave birth. Sometimes the offspring were functional. The Bloi triplets had been born in the kage. They didn't have too much neck and their arms were long, but they were quick, bright ten-year-olds now. And 2-Bloi and 3-Bloi are almost as dexterous with their feet as I am. I'd even given Lo 3-Bloi a couple of lessons on my blade, but being a child he preferred to pick fruit with his brothers.

After an hour in the dark, thinking about what went into the kage, what came out, I went back to the village, curled up on the haystack behind the smithy, and listened to the hum from the power-shack until it put me to sleep.

At dawn I unraveled, rubbed night's grit out of my eyes, and went to the corral. Easy and Little Jon got there a few minutes after. "Need any help with the goats this morning?"

Little Jon put his tongue in his cheek. "Just a second," he said and went off into the corner.

Easy shuffled uncomfortably.

Little Jon came back. "Yeah," he said. "Sure we need help." Then he grinned. And Easy, seeing his grin, grinned too.

Surprise! Surprise, little ball of fear inside me! They're smiling! Easy hoisted up the first bar of the wooden gate and the goats bleated forward and put their chins over the second rung. Surprise!

"Sure," Easy said. "Of course we need you. Glad to have you back!" He cuffed the back of my head and I swiped at his hip and missed. Little Jon pulled out the other rung, and we chased the goats across the square out along the road, and then up the meadow. Just like before. No, not just.

Easy said it first, when the first warmth pried under the dawn chill. "It's not just like before, Lobey. You've lost something."

I struck a dew shower from low willow fronds and wet my face and shoulders. "My appetite," I said. "And maybe a couple of pounds."

"It isn't your appetite," Little Jon said, coming back from a tree stump. "It's something different."

"Different?" I repeated. "Say, Easy, Little Jon, how am I different?"

"Huh?" Little Jon asked. He flung a stick at a goat to get its attention. Missed. I picked up a small stone that happened underfoot. Hit it. The goat turned blue eyes on me and gal-umphed over to see why, got interested in something else half-way over and tried to eat it. "You got big feet," Little Jon said.

"Naw. Not that," I said. "La Dire had noticed something different about me that's important; something different about me the same way there was about . . . Friza."

"You make music," Easy said.

I looked at the perforated blade. "Naw," I said. "I don't think it's that. I could teach you to play. That's another sort of being different than she's looking for. I think."

Late that afternoon we brought the goats back. Easy in-vited me to eat and I got some of my ham and we attacked Little Jon's cache of fruit. "You want to cook?"

"Naw," I said.

So Easy walked down to the corner of the power-shack and called towards the square, "Hey, who wants to cook dinner for three hard-working gentlemen who can supply food, en-tertainment, bright conversation—No, you cooked dinner for me once before. Now don't *push*, girls! Not you either. Whoever taught you how to season? Uh-uh, I remember you, Strychnine Lizzy. O.K. Yeah, you. Come on."

He came back with a cute, bald girl. I'd seen her around but she'd just come to the village. I'd never talked to her and I didn't know her name. "This is Little Jon, Lobey, and I'm Easy. What's your name again?"

"Call me Nativia."

No, I'd never talked to her before. A shame that situation had gone on for twenty-three years. Her voice didn't come from her larynx. I don't think she had one. The sound began a whole lot further down and whispered as out from a cave with bells.

"You can call me anything you like," I said, "as much as you want."

She laughed, and it sounded among the bells. "Where's the food and let's find a fireplace."

We found a circle of rocks down by the stream. We were going to get cookery from the compound but Nativia had a large skillet of her own so all we had to borrow were cinnamon and salt.

"Come on," Little Jon said when he came back from the water's edge. "Lobey, you gotta be entertaining. We'll converse."

"Now, hey—" Then I said to myself *Aw, so what*, lay down on my back, and began to play my machete. She liked that because she kept smiling at me as she worked.

"Don't you got no children?" Easy asked.

Nativia was greasing the skillet with a lump of ham fat.

"One in the kage down at Live Briar. Two with a man in Ko."

"You travel a lot, yeah?" Little Jon asked.

I played a slower tune that came far away, and she smiled at me as she dumped diced meat from a palm frond into the pan. Fat danced on the hot metal.

"I travel." The smile and the wind and the mockery in her voice were delightful.

"You should find a man who travels too," Easy suggested. He has a lot of homey type advice for everybody. Gets on my nerves sometimes.

Nativia shrugged. "Did once. We could never agree what direction to go in. It's his kid in the kage. Guy's name was Lo Angel. A beautiful man. He could just never make up his mind where he wanted to go. And when did, it was never where I wanted. No . . ." She pushed the browning meat across the crackling bottom. "I like good, stable, settled men who'll be there when I get back."

I began to play an old hymn—*Bill Bailey Won't You Please Come Home*. I'd learned it from a 45 when I was a kid. Nativia knew it too because she laughed in the middle of slicing a peach.

"That's me," she said. "Bill La Bailey. That's the nickname Lo Angel gave me."

She formed the meat into a ring around the edge of the

pan. The nuts and vegetables went in now with a little salt water, and the cover clanked on.

"How far have you traveled?" I asked, laying my knife on my stomach and stretching. Overhead, behind maple leaves, the sky was injured in the west with sunset, shadowed by east and night. "I'm going to travel soon. I want to know where there is to go."

She pushed the fruit on to one end of the frond. "I once went as far as the City. And I've even been underground to explore the source-cave."

Easy and Little Jon got very quiet.

"That's some traveling," I said. "La Dire says I have to travel because I'm different."

Nativia nodded. "That's why Lo Angel was traveling," she said, pushing back the lid again. Pungent steam ballooned and dispersed. My mouth got wet. "Most of the ones moving were different. He always said I was different too, but he would never tell me how." She pushed the vegetables into a ring against the meat and filled the center with cut fruit. Cinnamon now over the whole thing. Some of the powdered spice caught the flame that tongued the pan's rim and sparks bloomed. On went the cover.

"Yeah," I said. "La Dire won't tell me either."

Nativia looked surprised. "You mean you don't know?"

I shook my head.

"Oh, but you can—" She stopped. "La Dire is one of this town's elders, isn't she?"

"That's right."

"Maybe she's got a reason not to tell you. I talked to her just a little while the other day; she's a woman of great wisdom."

"Yeah," I said, rolling on my side. "Come on, if you know, tell me."

Nativia looked confused. "Well, first you tell me. I mean what did La Dire say?"

"She said I would have to go on a journey, to kill whatever killed Friza."

"Friza?"

"Friza was different, too." I began to tell her the story. A minute into it, Easy burped, pounded his chest, and complained about being hungry. He obviously didn't like the subject. Little Jon had to get up and when he wandered off into the bushes, Easy went after him, grunting, "Call me when it's finished. Dinner, I mean."

But Nativia listened closely and then asked some questions about Friza's death. When I told her about having to take a trip with Le Dorik, she nodded. "Well, it makes a lot more sense now."

"It does?"

She nodded again. "Hey, you guys, dinner's . . . ready?"

"Then can't you tell me . . . ?"

She shook her head. "You wouldn't understand. I've done a lot more traveling than you. It's just that a lot of different people have died recently, like Friza died. Two down at Live Briar. And I've heard of three more in the past year. Something is going to have to be done. It might as well get started here." She pushed the cover off the pan again: more steam.

Easy and Little Jon, who had been walking back up the stream, began to run.

"Elvis Presley!" Little Jon breathed. "Does that smell good!" He hunkered down by the fire, dribbling.

Easy's adenoids began to rattle. When a cat does it, it's purring.

I wanted to ask more, but I didn't want to annoy Easy and Little Jon; I guess I had acted bad with them, and they were pretty nice about it as long as I let it lie.

A frond full of ham, vegetables, and spiced fruit made me stop thinking about anything except what wasn't in my belly, and I learned that a good deal of my metaphysical melancholia was hunger. Always is.

More conversation, more food, more entertainment. We went to sleep right there by the stream, stretched on the ferns. Towards midnight when it got chilly we rolled into a pile. About an hour before dawn I woke.

I pulled my head from Easy's armpit (and Nativia's bald head moved immediately to take its place) and stood up in the starry dark. Little Jon's head gleamed at my feet. So did my blade. He was using it for a pillow. I slipped it gently from under his cheek. He snorted, scratched himself, was still. I started back through the trees in the direction of the kage.

Once I looked up at the branches, at the wires that ran from the power-shack to the fence. The black lines overhead, or the sound of the stream, or memory took me. Halfway, I started playing. Someone began to whistle along with me. I stopped. The whistle didn't.

Where is he then? In a song?   Jean Genet, *The Screens*

God said to Abraham, "Kill me a son."
Abe said, "God, you must be puttin' me on!"
    Bob Dylan, "Highway 61 Revisited"

Love is something which dies and when dead it rots and
becomes soil for a new love . . . Thus in reality there is
no death in love.   Par Lagerkvist, *The Dwarf*

"Le Dorik?" I said. "Dorik?"

"Hi," came a voice from the dark. "Lobey?"

"Lo Lobey," I said. "Where are you?"

"Just inside the kage."

"Oh. What's the smell?"

"Whitey," Dorik said. "Easy's brother. He died. I'm digging
a grave. You remember Easy's brother—"

"I remember," I said. "I saw him by the fence yesterday. He
looked pretty sick."

"That kind never last long. Come in and help me dig."

"The fence . . ."

"It's off. Climb over."

"I don't like to go in the kage," I said.

"You never used to mind sneaking in here when we were
kids. Come on, I've got to move this rock. Lend me a foot."

"That was when we were kids," I said. "We did a lot of
things when we were kids we don't have to do now. It's your
job. You dig."

"Friza used to come in here and help me, tell me all about
you."

"Friza used to . . ." Then I said, "Tell?"

"Well, some of us could understand her."

"Yeah," I said. "Some of us could."

I grabbed the wire mesh near the post but didn't start climbing.

"Actually," Dorik said, "I was always sort of sad you never came around. We used to have fun. I'm glad Friza didn't feel the way you did. We used to—"

"—to do a lot of things, Dorik. Yeah, I know. Look, nobody ever bothered to tell me you weren't a girl till I was fourteen, Dorik. If I hurt you, I'm sorry."

"You did. But I'm not. Nobody ever did get around to telling Friza I wasn't a boy. Which I'm sort of glad of. I don't think she would have taken it the same way you did, even so."

"She came here a lot?"

"All the time she wasn't with you."

I sprang over the wire, swung over the top, and dropped to the other side. "Where's that damn rock you're trying to move?"

"Here—"

"Don't touch me," I said. "Just show me."

"Here," Dorik repeated in the darkness.

I grabbed the edge of the stone shelved in the dirt. Roots broke, dirt whispered down, and I rolled the stone out.

"How's the kid, by the way?" I asked.

I had to. And damn, Dorik, why were the next words the ones I was hurting with hoping I wouldn't hear?

"Which one?"

There was a shovel by the post. I jammed it into the grave. Damn Le Dorik.

"Mine and Friza's," Dorik went on after a moment, "will probably be up for review by the doctors in another year. Needs a lot of special training, but she's pretty functional. Probably will never have a La, but at least she won't have to be in here."

"That's not the kid I meant." The shovel clanged on another rock.

"You're not asking about the one that's all mine." There were two or three pieces of ice in that sentence. Dorik flicked them at me, much on purpose. "You mean yours and mine." As if you didn't know, you androgynous bastard. "He's in here for life, but he's happy. Want to go see him—"

"No." Three more shovelsful of dirt. "Let's bury Whitey and get out of here."

"Where are we going?"

"La Dire, she said you and me have to take a trip together to destroy what killed Friza."

"Oh," Dorik said. "Yes." Dorik went over to the fence, bent down. "Help me."

We picked up the bloated, rubbery corpse and carried it to the hole. It rolled over the edge, thumping.

"You were supposed to wait till I came for you," Dorik said.

"Yeah. But I can't wait. I want to go now."

"If I'm going with you, you're waiting."

"Why?"

"Look, Lobey," Dorik said, "I'm kage-keeper and I got a kage to keep."

"I don't care if everything in that kage mildews and rots. I want to get out and get going!"

"I've got to train a new keeper, check over the education facilities, make sure of the food inventories and special diets, last minute shelter maintenance—"

"Damn it, Dorik, come on."

"Lobey, I've got three kids in here. One's yours, one belongs to a girl you loved. And one's all mine. Two of them, if they're loved and taken care of and given a lot of time and patience may someday come out."

"Two of them, yeah?" My breath suddenly got lost in my chest and didn't seem to be doing any good. "But not mine. I'm going."

"Lobey!"

I stopped, straddling the fence.

"Look, Lobey, this is the real world you're living in. It's come from something; it's going to something: it's changing.

But it's got right and wrong, a way to behave and a way not to. You never wanted to accept that, even when you were a kid, but until you do, you won't be very happy."

"You're talking about me when I was fourteen," I said.

"I'm talking about you now. Friza told me a lot—"

I jumped over the fence and started through the trees.

"Lobey!"

"What?" I kept walking.

"You're scared of me."

"No."

"I'll show you—"

"You're pretty good at showing people things in the dark, aren't you? That's how you're different, huh?" I called over my shoulder. I crossed the stream and started up the rocks, mad as all Elvis. I didn't go towards the meadow, but around towards the steeper places, slapping leaves and flipping twigs as I barreled through the dark. Then I heard somebody come on through the shadow, whistling.

There are none here except madmen; and a few there are who know this world, and who know that he who tries to act in the ways of others never does anything, because men never have the same opinions. These do not know that he who is thought wise by day will never be held crazy by night.

Niccolo Machiavelli, "Letter to Francesco Vittori"

Experience reveals to him in every object, in every event, the presence of *something* else.

Jean-Paul Sartre, *Saint Genet, Actor and Martyr*

I stopped. The sound of dry leaves under feet, ferns by a shoulder, approached me from behind, stopped. The hills' rim had begun to gray.

"Lobey?"

"You changed your mind about coming?"

A sigh. "Yes."

"Come on, then." We started walking. "Why?"

"Something happened."

Dorik didn't say what. I didn't ask.

"Dorik," I said a little later, "I feel something towards you very close to hate. It's as close to hate as what I felt for Friza was close to love."

"Neither's close enough to worry about now. You're too self-centered, Lobey. I hope you grow up."

"And you're going to show me how?" I asked. "In the dark?"

"I'm showing you now."

Morning, while we walked, leaked up vermilion. With light, my eyes grew surprisingly heavy, stones in my head. "You've been working all night," I volunteered. "I've only had a few hours sleep myself. Why don't we lie down for a few hours?"

"Wait till it gets light enough so you know I'm here." Which was an odd answer. Dorik was a grayed silhouette beside me now.

When there was enough red in the east and the rest of the sky was at least blue, I started looking for a place to fall out. I was exhausted and every time I turned to look at the sun, the world swam with tears of fatigue.

"Here," Dorik said. We'd reached a small stone hollow by the cliff's base. I dropped into it, Dorik too. We lay with the blade between us. I remember a moment of gold light along the arm and back curved towards me before I slept.

I touched the hand touching my face, held it still enough to open my eyes under it. Lids snapped back. "Dorik—?"

Nativia stared down at me.

My fingers intertwined with hers, hammocked by her webs. She looked frightened, and her breath through spread lips stopped my own. "Easy!" she called up the slope. "Little Jon! Here he is!"

I sat up. "Where'd Dorik go . . . ?"

Easy came loping into sight and Little Jon ran after.

"La Dire," Easy said. "La Dire wants to see you . . . before you go. She and Lo Hawk have to talk to you."

"Hey, did anybody see Le Dorik around here? Odd thing to run off—"

Then I saw this expression cracking through Little Jon's miniature features like faults in black rock. "Le Dorik's dead," Little Jon said; "that's what they wanted to tell you."

"Huh?"

"Before sunup, just inside the kage," Easy said. "He was lying by the grave for my brother, Whitey. Remember my brother—"

"Yeah, yeah," I said. "I helped dig it—Before sunup? That's impossible. The sun was up when we went to sleep, right here." Then I said, "Dead?"

Little Jon nodded. "Like Friza. The same way. That's what La Dire said."

I stood up, holding my blade tight. "But that's impossible!" Somebody saying, *Wait till it gets light enough so you'll know I'm here.* "Le Dorik was with me after sunrise. That's when we lay down here to sleep."

"You slept with Le Dorik *after* Le Dorik was dead?" Nativia asked, wonderingly.

Bewildered, I returned to the village. La Dire and Lo Hawk met me at the source-cave. We spoke together a bit; I watched them thinking deeply about things I didn't understand, about my bewilderment.

"You're a good hunter, Lo Lobey," Lo Hawk said at last, "and though a bit outsized below the waist, a fair specimen of a man. You have much danger ahead of you; I've taught you much. Remember it when you wander by the rim of night or the edge of morning." Apparently Le Dorik's death had convinced him there was something to La Dire's suppositions, though I understood neither side of the argument nor the bridge between. They didn't enlighten me. "Use what I have taught you to get where you are going," Lo Hawk went on, "to survive your stay, and make your way back."

"You are different." That is what La Dire said. "You have seen it is dangerous to be so. It is also very important. I have tried to instruct you in a view of the world large enough to encompass the deeds you will do as well as their significance. You have learned much, Lo Lobey. Use what I have taught you too."

With no idea where I was going, I turned and staggered away, still dazed by Dorik's death before sunrise. Apparently the Bloi triplets had been up all night fishing for blind-crabs in the mouth of the source-cave stream. They'd come back while it was still dark, swinging their hand-beams and joking as they walked up from the river—Dorik behind the wire in a net of shadow, circled with their lights, face down at the grave's edge! It must have been just moments after I first left.

I wheeled through the brambles, heading toward noon, with one thought clearing, as figures on a stream bed clear when you brush back the bubbles a moment: if Le Dorik, dead, had walked with me a while ("I'm showing you now, Lobey"), walked through dawn and gorse, curled on a stone under new sunlight, then Friza too could travel with me. If I could find what killed those of us who were different, but whose difference gave us a reality beyond dying—

A slow song now on my blade to mourn Dorik; and the beat of my feet on earth in journey. After a few hours of such mourning, the heat had polished me with sweat as in some funeral dance.

While day leaned over the hills I passed the first red flowers, blossoms big as my face, like blood bubbles nestled in thorns, often resting on the bare rock. No good to stop here. Carnivorous.

I squatted on a broken seat of granite in the yellowing afternoon. A snail the size of my curled forefinger bobbed his eyes at a puddle big as my palm. Half an hour later, climbing down a canyon wall when yellow had died under violet, I saw a tear in the rock: another opening into the source-cave. I decided on nighting it there, and ducked in.

Still smells of humans and death. Which is good. Dangerous animals avoid it. I stalked inside, padding on all fours. Loose earth became moss, became cement underfoot. Outside, night, sonic lace of crickets and whining wasps I would not make on my knife, was well into black development.

Soon I touched a metal track, turned, and followed it with my hands . . . over a place where dirt had fallen, across a scattering of twigs and leaves, then down a long slope. I was about to stop, roll against the cave wall where it was drier, and sleep, when the track split.

I stood up.

When I shrilled on my blade, a long echo came from the right: endless passage there. But only a stubby resonance from the left: some sort of chamber. I walked left. My hip brushed a door jamb.

Then a room glowed suddenly before me. The sensor circuits were still sensitive. Grilled walls, blue glass desk, brass light fixtures, cabinets, and a television screen set in the wall. Squinting in the new light, I walked over. When they still work, the colors are nice to watch: they make patterns and the patterns make music in me. Several people who had gone exploring the source-cave had told me about them (night fire and freakishly interested children knotted around the flame and the adventurer), and I'd gone to see one in a well explored arm two years back. Which is how I learned about the music.

Color television is certainly a lot more fun than this terribly risky genetic method of reproduction we've taken over. Ah well. It's a lovely world.

I sat on the desk and tried knobs till one clicked. The screen grayed at me, flickered, streamed with colors.

There was static, so I found the volume knob and turned it down . . . so I could hear the music in the colors. Just as I raised my blade to my mouth, something happened.

Laughter.

First I thought it was melody. But it was a voice laughing. And on the screen, in chaotic shimmerings, a face. It wasn't a picture of a face. It was as if I was just looking at the particular dots of melody/hue that formed the face, ignoring the rest. I would have seen those features on any visual riot: Friza's face.

The voice was someone else's.

Friza dissolved. Another face replaced hers: Dorik's. The strange laughter again. Suddenly there was Friza on one side of the screen, and Dorik on the other. Centered: the boy who was laughing at me. The picture cleared, filled, and I lost the rest of the room. Behind him, crumbled streets, beams jutting from the wrecks of walls, weeds writhing; and all lit with flickering green, the sun white on the reticulated sky. On a lamp-post behind him perched a creature with fins and white gills, scraping one red foot on the rust. On the curb was a hydrant laced with light and verdigris.

The boy, a redhead—redder than the Blois, redder than

blood-glutted blossoms—laughed with downcast eyes. His lashes were gold. Transparent skin caught up the green and fluoresced with it; but I knew that under normal light he would have been as pale as Whitey dying.

"Lobey," in the laughter, and his lips uncurtained small teeth—many too many of them. Like the shark's mouth, maybe, I'd seen in La Dire's book, rank on rank of ivory needles. "Lobey, how you gonna find me, huh?"

"What . . . ?" and expected the illusion to end with my voice.

But somewhere that naked, laughing boy still stood with one foot in the gutter filled with waving weeds. Only Friza and Dorik were gone.

"Where are you?"

He looked up and his eyes had no whites, only glittering gold and brown. I'd seen a few like that before, eyes. Unnerving, still, to look at a dog's eyes in a human face. "My mother called me Bonny William. Now they all call me Kid Death." He sat on the curb, hanging his hands over his knees. "You're gonna find me, Lobey, kill me like I killed Friza and Dorik?"

"You? You, Lo Bonny William—"

"No Lo. Kid Death. Not Lo Kid."

"You *killed* them? But . . . *why?*" Despair unvoiced my words to whispers.

"Because they were different. And I am more different than any of you. You scare me, and when I'm frightened"—laughing again—"I kill." He blinked. "You're not looking for me, you know. I'm looking for you."

"What do you mean?"

He shook shocked crimson from his white brow. "I'm bringing you down here to me. If I didn't want you, you'd never find me. Because I do want you, there's no way you can avoid me. I can see through the eyes of anyone on this world, on any world where our ancestors have ever been: so I know a lot about many things I've never touched or smelled. You've started out not knowing where I am and running towards me.

You'll end, Lo Lobey"—he raised his head—"fleeing my green home, scrabbling on the sand like a blind goat trying to keep footing at a chimney edge, and—"

"—how do you know about—"

"—you'll fall and break your neck." He shook a finger at me, clawed like Little Jon's. "Come to me, Lo Lobey."

"If I find you, will you give me back Friza?"

"I've already given you back Le Dorik for a little while."

"*Can* you give me back Friza?"

"Everything I kill I keep. In my own private kage." His moist laughter. Water in a cold pipe, I think.

"Kid Death?"

"What?"

"Where are you?"

The sound snagged on ivory needles.

"Where are you from, Kid Death? Where are you going?"

The long fingers raveled like linen rope snaring gold coins. He pushed weeds away from the gutter grill with his foot. "I broiled away childhood in the sands of an equatorial desert kage with no keeper to love me. Like you, lively in your jungle, I was haunted by the memories of those who homed under this sun before our parents' parents came, took on these bodies, loves, and fears. Most of those around me in the kage died of thirst. At first I saved some of my fellows, bringing water to them the way Friza threw the stone—oh yes, I saw that too. I did that for a while. Then for a while I killed whoever was put in the kage with me, and took the water directly from their bodies. I would go to the fence and stare across the dunes to the palms at the oasis where our tribe worked. I never thought to leave the kage, back then, because like mirages on the glistering I saw through all the worlds' eyes—I saw what you and Friza and Dorik saw, as I see what goes all over this arm of the galaxy. When what I saw frightened me, I closed the eyes seeing. That's what happened to Friza and Dorik. When I am still curious about what's going on through those eyes, more curious than frightened, I open them again. That's what happened with Dorik."

"You're strong," I said.

"That's where I come from, the desert, where death shifts in the gritty bones of the Earth. And now? I am going further and further into the sea." Raising his eyes now, his red hair floated back in the shivering green.

"Kid Death," I called again; he was much further away. "Why were you in the kage? You look more functional than half the Lo and La of my village."

Kid Death turned his head and looked at me from the corner of his eyes. He mocked. "Functional? To be born on a desert, a white-skinned redhead with gills?"

The spreading, drinking, miniature mouth of the shark washed away. I blinked. I couldn't think of anything else so I took papers out of the filing cabinet, spread them under the desk, and lay down, tired and bewildered.

I remember I picked up one page and spelled my way through a paragraph. La Dire had taught me enough to read record labels, when for a while I had foraged about the village archives:

Evacuate upper levels with all due haste. Alarm system will indicate radiation at standard levels. Deeper detection devices are located . . .

Most of the words were beyond me. I halved the paper with toes and quartered it with fingers, let the pieces fall on my stomach before I picked up my machete to play myself to sleep.

What, then, is noble abstraction? It is taking first the essential elements of the thing to be represented, then the rest in the order of importance (so that wherever we pause we shall always have obtained more than we leave behind) and using any expedient to impress what we want upon the mind without caring about the mere literal accuracy of such expedient.

John Ruskin, *The Stones of Venice*

A poem is a machine for making choices.

John Ciardi, *How Does a Poem Mean*

Hours after—I figure it could have been two, it could have been twelve—I rolled from under the desk and came up grunting, yawning, scratching. When I stepped into the hall the light faded.

I didn't go back the way I'd come but headed forward again. There are lots of breakthroughs into the upper levels. I'd go till I saw morning and climb out. About half an hour later I see a three-foot stretch of it (morning) in the ceiling, behind black leaves, and leap for it. Good jumping power in those hams.

I scrambled out on crumbling ground and tame brambles, tripped on a vine, but all in all did pretty well. Which is to avoid saying "on the whole." Outside was cool, misty. Fifty yards by, the lapping edge of a lake flashed. I walked through the tangle to the clear beach. Chunked rock became gravel, became sand. It was a big lake. Down one arm of the beach things faded into reeds and swamp and things. Across, there was a gorse covered plain. I had no idea where I was. But I didn't want to be in a swamp, so I walked up the other way.

Thrash, thrash, *snap!*

I stopped.

Thrash! Just inside the jungle something churned and fought. The fighting was at the point where one opponent was near exhausted: activity came in momentary spurts. (*Hissssss!*) Curiosity, hunger, devilment sent me forward with high machete. I crept up a slope of rock, looked over into a glade.

Attacked by flowers, a dragon was dying. Blossoms jeweled his scales; thorns tangled his legs. As I watched, he tried again to tear them off with his teeth, but they scurried back, raking briars across his hide, or whipping them at his runny, yellow eyes.

The lizard (twice as big as Easy and man-branded on his left hinder haunch with a crusty cross) was trying to protect the external gill/lung arrangement that fluttered along his neck. The plants had nearly immobilized him, but when a bloom advanced to tear away his breath, he scraped and flailed with one free claw. He'd mauled a good many of the blossoms and their petals scattered the torn earth.

The cross told me he wouldn't hurt me (even crazed, the lizard once used to man becomes pathetic, seldom harmful) so I jumped down from the rock.

A blossom creeping to attack emptied an air-bladder inches from my foot, "*Sssssss . . .*" in surprise.

I hacked it, and nervous ooze (nervous in the sense that its nerves are composed of the stuff) belched greenly to the ground. Thorns flailed my legs. But I told you about the skin down there. I just have to watch out for my belly and the palms of my hands; feet are fine. With my foot I seized a creeper from the lizard's shoulder and pulled it out far enough—stained teeth go *clik-clik-clik* popping from the dragon's skin where they had been gnawing—to get my blade under, twist . . . and . . . *rip!*

Nerve dribbled the dragon's hide.

Those flowers communicate somehow (differently perhaps) and strove for me, one suddenly rising on its tendrils and leaping, "*Ssssss . . .*" I twiddled my blade in its brain.

I shouted encouragement to the dragon, threw a brave grin. He moaned reptilianly. Lo Hawk should see me do proud his skill.

His mane brushed my arm, his teeth crunched a flower while tendrils curled from the corners of his mouth. He chewed a while, decided he didn't like it, spat thorns. I pried off two more: his foot came free.

"*Ssssss . . .*" I looked to the right.

Which was a mistake because it was coming from the left.

Mistakes like that are a drag. Long and prickly wrapped my ankle and tried to jerk me off my feet. Fortunately you just can't do that. So then it sank lots of teeth into my calf and commenced chewing. I whirled and snatched white petals (this one an albino) which came away gently in my hand. *Crunch, Crunch,* still on my calf. My sword hand was up. I brought it down but it got caught in a net of brambles. Something scratched the back of my neck. Which ain't so tough.

Neither is (come to think): the small of my back, under my chin, between my legs, armpits, behind my ears—I was quickly cataloging all the tender places now. Damn flowers move just slow enough to give you time to think.

Then something long and hot sang by my shins. Petals snapped into the air. The plant stopped chewing and burped nervously down my ankle.

Pinnnnng near my hand, and my hand pulled free. I staggered, hacked another briar away. A bloated rose slithered down the dragon's leg and crawled for cover. They communicate, yes, and the communication was *fear* and *retreat*. The music, though! Lord, the *music!*

I whirled to look up on the rock.

Morning had got far enough along to rouge the sky behind him. He flicked a final encumbering flower from the beast, "*Ssssss . . . blop!*" and coiled his whip. I rubbed my calf. The dragon moaned, off key.

"Yours?" I thumbed over my shoulder at the beast.

"Was." He breathed deeply and the flat, bony chest sagged

with his breathing, the ribs opening and closing like blinds. "If you come with us, he's yours—to ride, anyway. If you don't, he's mine again."

The dragon rubbed his gills ingenuously against my hip.

"Can you handle a dragon whip?" the stranger asked me.

I shrugged. "The only time I ever even saw one of those before was when some herders got off their trail six years ago." We'd all climbed up Beryl Face and watched them drive the herd of lizards back through Green-glass Pass. When Lo Hawk went to talk to them, I went with him, which is where I found out about branding and the gentle monsters.

The stranger grinned. "Well, it's gone and happened again. I judge we're about twenty-five kilometers off. You want a job and a lizard to ride?"

I looked at the broken flowers. "Yeah."

"Well, there's your mount, and your job is to get him up here and back with the herd, first."

"Oh." (Now, lemme see; I remember the herders perched behind the lumps of the beasts' shoulders with their feet sort of tucked into the scaly armpits. My feet? And holding on to the two white whisker type things that grew back from the gills: Gee . . . Haw? Giddiap!)

We floundered in the mud about fifteen minutes with instructions shouted down, and I learned cuss words I hadn't ever heard from that guy. Towards the end we were both sort of laughing. The dragon was up and on the beach now, and he had quite unintentionally thrown me into the water—again.

"Hey, you think I'm really going to learn how to ride that thing?"

With one hand he was helping me up, with the other he was holding my mount by the whiskers, with another he was recoiling his whip, and with the fourth he just scratched his woolly head. "Don't give up. I didn't do too much better when I started. Up you go."

Up I went, and stayed on this time for a staggering run up and down the water's edge. I mean it looks graceful enough from the ground. It *feels* like staggering. On stilts.

"You're getting the hang of it."

"Thanks," I said. "Say, where is the herd; and who are you?"

He stood ankle deep in the lake's lapping. Morning was bright enough now to gem his chest and shoulders with drops from my splashing. He smiled and wiped his face. "Spider," he said. "And I didn't catch your name . . . ?"

"Lo Lobey." I rocked happily behind the scaly hump.

"Don't say Lo to nobody herding," said Spider. "No need for it."

"Wouldn't even have thought of it if it weren't for my village ways," I said.

"Herd's off that way." He swung up behind me on the dragon.

Amber haired, four handed, and slightly hump-backed, Spider was seven feet of bone slipped into six feet of skin. Tightly. All tied in with long, narrow muscles. He was burned red, and the red burned brown but still glowing through. And he laughed like dry leaves crushed inside his chest. We circled the lake silently. And, oh man, the music!

The herd, maybe two hundred and fifty dragons moaning about (I was to learn that this was a happy sound), milled in a dell beyond the lake. Youth had romanticized the herders in my memory. They were motley. I see why you don't go around Lo-ing and La-ing and Le-ing herders. Two of them—I *still* don't see how they managed to stay on their dragons. But I came on friendly.

One kid with a real mind: you could tell by the way his green eye glittered at you, as well as his whip skill, and the sure way he handled dragons. Only he was mute. Was it this that upset me and made me think of Friza? You have a job to do. . . .

There was another guy who would have made Whitey look like a total norm. He had some glandular business that made him smell bad too. And he wanted to tell me his life story (no motor control of the mouth so he sort of splattered when he got excited).

I wish Green-eye could have talked instead of Stinky. I

wanted to learn where he'd been, what he'd seen—he knew some good songs.

Dragons get lost at night. So you round them up in the morning. I'd been rounded up along with the stray animals. At breakfast I gathered from Stinky that I was a replacement for somebody who had come to a bad, sad, and messy end the previous afternoon.

"Oddest people survive out here," Spider mused. "Oddest ones don't. She looked a lot more 'normal' than you. But she ain't here now. Just goes to show you."

Green-eye blinked at me from under all his black hair, caught me watching him, and went back to splicing his whip.

"When are those dragon eggs gonna finish baking?" Knife asked, pawing at the fireplace stones with gray hands.

Spider kicked at him and the herder scuttled away. "Wait till we all eat." But in a few minutes he crawled back and was rubbing against the stones. "Warm," he muttered apologetically, when Spider started to kick him again. "I like it warm."

"Just keep off the food."

"Where do you take these to?" I indicated the herd. "Where do you bring them from?"

"They breed in the Hot Swamp, about two hundred kilometers west of here. We drive them down this way, across the Great City and on to Branning-at-sea. There the sterile ones are slaughtered; the eggs are removed from the females, inseminated, then we bring the eggs back and plant them in the swamp."

"Branning-at-sea?" I asked. "What do they do with them there?"

"Eat most. Use others for work. It's quite a fantastic place for someone born in the woods, I would imagine. I've been back and forth so many times it's like home. I've got a house and a wife and three kids there, and another family back in the Swamp."

We ate eggs, fried lizard fat, and thick cereal, hot and filling, with plenty of salt and chopped peppers. When I finished I began to play my blade.

That *music!*

It was a whole lot of tunes at once, many the same, but starting at different times. I had to pick one strand out and play it. A few notes into it, I saw Spider staring at me, surprised. "Where did you hear that?" he asked.

"Just made it up, I guess."

"Don't be silly."

"It was just running around my head. All confused, though."

"Play it again, Sam—"

I did. This time Spider began to whistle one of the other melodies that went along with it so that they glittered and jumped against each other.

When we finished he said, "You're different, aren't you?"

"So I've been told," I said. "Say, what's the name of that song anyway? It's not like most of the music I know."

"It's the Kodaly 'Sonata for Unaccompanied Cello.'"

Morning wind shook the gorse. "The *what?*" I asked. Behind us dragons moaned.

"You got it out of my head?" Spider said questioningly. "You couldn't have heard it before unless I was going around humming. And I can't hum a crescendo of triple stops."

"I got it from you?"

"That music's been going through my mind for weeks. Heard it at a concert last summer at Branning-at-sea, the night before I left to take the eggs back to the swamp. Then I discovered an LP of the piece in the music section of the ruins of the ancient library at Haifa."

"I learned it from you?" and suddenly all sorts of things cleared up, like how La Dire knew I was different, like how Nativia could tell I was different when I started playing *Bill Bailey.* "Music," I said. "So that's where I get my music from." I put the blade's tip on the ground and leaned on it.

Spider shrugged.

"I don't think I get all of it from other people," I said, frowning. "Different?" I ran my thumb along the blade's edge and skipped my toes over the holes.

"I'm different too," Spider said.

"How?"

"Like this." He closed his eyes and all his shoulders knotted. My machete jerked from my hand, pulled from the ground, and spun in the air. Then it fell point first to quiver in the shank of a log near the fire. Spider opened his eyes and took a breath.

My mouth was open. So I closed it.

Everybody else thought it was very funny.

"And with animals," Spider said.

"How?"

"The dragons. To a certain point I can keep them calm, keep them more or less together, and steer dangerous creatures away from us."

"Friza," I said. "You're like Friza."

"Who's Friza?"

I looked down at my knife. The melody which I had mourned her with was mine. "Nobody," I said, "anymore." That melody was mine! Then I asked, "Have you ever heard of Kid Death?"

Spider put down his food, brought all his hands in front of him, and tilted his head. His long nostrils flared till they were round. I looked away from his fear. But the others were watching me so I had to look back.

"What about Kid Death?" Spider asked.

"I want to find him and—" I flung my blade in the air and twirled it as Spider had, but my hand had propelled it. I seized it from its fall with my foot. "—Well, I want to find him. Tell me about him."

They laughed. It started in Spider's mouth, then was coming all sloppy from Stinky, a low hiss from Knife, grunts and cackles from the others, ending in Green-eye's green eye, a light that went out as he looked away. "You're going to have a hard time," Spider said finally, "but"—he rose from the fire—"you're headed in the right direction."

"Tell me about him," I said again.

"There's a time to talk about the impossible, but it's not

when there's work to do." He got up, reached into a canvas sack, and tossed me a whip.

I caught it mid-length.

"Put your ax away," Spider said. "This sings when it flies." His lash lisped over my head.

Everyone went to his mount, and Spider reeled a bridle and stirrups from the gear sack that fitted those humps and scales neatly, buckling around the forelegs; I see why he'd made me get the feel of things bareback. The semi-saddle and leg-straps make dragon riding almost nice.

"Head them on through that way," he yelled, and I imitated the herders around me as they began the drive.

Dragons swarmed in sunlight.

Oiled whips snapped and glistened over the scales, and the whole world got caught up in the rhythmic rocking of the beast between my legs, trees and hills and gorse and boulders and brambles all taking up the tune and movement as a crowd will begin clapping and stomping to a beat; the jungle, my audience, applauded the beat of surging lizards.

Moaning. Which meant they were happy.

Hissing sometimes. Which meant watch it.

Grunting and cussing and shouting. Which meant the herders were happy too.

I learned an incredible amount of things that morning, lunging back and forth between the creatures: five or six of them were the leaders and the rest followed. Keep the leaders going in the right direction and you had no problem. Dragons tend to go right. You get more response if you slap them on the back haunches. I later learned, nerve clusters there control their rear-end transmissions that're bigger than the brain.

One of the lead dragons kept on wanting to go back and bother an overweight female (ovarian tumor that kept her loaded down with sterile eggs, Spider explained to me) and it was all we could do to keep them apart. I spent a lot of time (imitating Green-eye) scouting the edge of the herd to worry the creatures back together who kept getting curious about things in irrelevant directions.

I began to learn what I was doing when about twenty drag-ons got stuck in a mintbog. (A slushy, slow quicksand *bog* cov-ered with huge bushes of windy *mint*, right? Mintbog.) Spi-der, by himself drove the rest of the herd around in a circle, three whips popping, while the other five of us went sloshing back and forth through the mint to drive the dragons out be-fore they drowned.

"There shouldn't be too many more of those," Spider shouted when we were charging along again. "We'll be cross-ing the City in a little while if we're not too far off course. I've been swinging us westward."

My arm was sore.

Once I got twenty seconds of calm riding time beside Green-eye: "Isn't this a pretty stupid way to waste your life, fellow?"

He grinned.

Then two very friendly dragons came galumphing and moaning between us. Sweat slopped into my eyes and my armpits felt oiled. The harness made it a little easier on my inner thighs; they got raw slow 'stead of quick. I could hardly see and was playing it more by ear than eye when Spider called, "Back on course! City up ahead!"

I looked up but fresh sweat flooded my eyes and the heat made everything waver. I drove dragons. The gorse lessened, and we started down.

Earth crumbled under their claws. With no vegetation to blunt the temperature, the sun stuck gold needles in the backs of our necks. Reflected heat from the ground. At last, sand.

The dragons had to slow. Spider paused beside me to thumb sweat from his eyes. "We usually take McClellan Av-enue," he told me as he looked across the dunes. "But I think we're closer to Main Street. This hits McClellan a few miles out. We'll stop at the intersection and rest until nightfall." The dragons hissed out across the City sands. Swamp crea-tures, they were not used to this dryness. As we plowed the ancient place, silent and furious with hundreds of beasts, I remember crossing a moment of untimed horror, when through void buff I imagined myself surrounded of a sudden, crowded by millions, straited by walls, sooty, fuming, roaring with the dread, dead old race of the planet.

I flailed my whip and beat away the notion. The sun ground its light into the sand.

Two dragons began to annoy each other and I flicked them apart. They snatched at my lash indignantly, missed. My breath filed my throat. Yet, as the two moved away, I realized I was grinning. Alone, we toiled through the day, content and terrified.

Slipped from the night waters of the Adriatic and now we skirt down the strait towards the Piraeus. At the horizon right and left monstrously beautiful mountains gnaw the sky. The ship is easy on the morning. The speakers give up French, English, and Greek pop music. Sun silvers the hosed deck, burns over the smokestack. Bought deck passage; big and bold last night I walked into a cabin and slept beautifully. Back outside this morning I wonder what effect Greece will have on TEI. The central subject of the book is myth. This music is so appropriate for the world I float on. I was aware how well it fitted the capsulated life of New York. Its torn harmonies are even more congruent with the rest of the world. How can I take Lobey into the center of this bright chaos propelling these sounds? Drank late with the Greek sailors last night; in bad Italian and worse Greek we talked about myths. Taiki learned the story of Orpheus not from school or reading but from his aunt in Eleusis. Where shall I go to learn it? The sailors my age wanted to hear pop English and French music on the portable radio. The older ones wanted to hear the traditional Greek songs. "Demotic songs!" exclaimed Demo. "All the young men in the words want to die as soon as possible because love has treated them badly!"

"Not so with Orpheus," Taiki said, a little mysteriously, a little high.

Did Orpheus want to live after he lost Eurydice the second time? He had a very modern choice to make when he decided to look back. What is its musical essence?

Writer's Journal, Gulf of Corinth, November 1965

I drive fine dragons
for a fine dragon lord,
a lord of fine dragons
and his dragon horde

Green-eye sang that silently as we dropped from our mounts. For the first time in my life I caught words as well as melody. It surprised me and I turned to stare. But he was loosening the harness on his beast. The sky was blue glass. West, clouds smudged the evening with dirty yellow. The dragons threw long shadows on the sand. Coals glowed in the makeshift fireplace. Batt was cooking already.

"McClellan and Main," Spider said. "Here we are."

"How can you tell?" I asked.

"I've been here before."

"Oh."

The dragons had more or less decided we were really stopping. Many lay down.

My mount (whom I had inadvertently named something unprintable; a day's repetition had stabilized the monicker. Therefore we must call him: My Mount) nuzzled my neck affectionately, nearly knocked me down, then dropped his chin to the sand, folded his forelegs, and let his hinder parts fall where they might. That's how dragons do it. Sit down I mean.

Ten steps and I didn't think I would walk again. I tied my whip around my waist, went as close to the food as I could without stepping on anybody, and sat. The exhausted muscles of my legs sagged like water bags. Supplies and equipment were piled to one side. Spider lay down on top of them with one hand hanging down over the edge. I stared at his hand across the fire: because it was in front of me, that's all. And I learned a few things about Spider.

It was large, hung from a knobbly wrist. The skin between thumb and forefinger was cracked like stone, and the ridges of his knuckles were filled with sweat dampened dirt. A bar of callous banded the front of his palm before the abruptness of his fingers—that was all hard dragon work. But also, on the middle finger at the first knuckle was a callous facing the forefinger. That comes from holding a writing tool. La Dire has such a callous and I asked her about it once. Third, on the tips of his fingers (but not his thumb. It was a left hand) there were smooth shiny spots: those you get from playing a stringed instrument, guitar, violin . . . maybe cello? Sometimes when I play with other people I notice them. So Spider herds dragons. And he writes. And he plays music . . .

While I sat there, it occurred to me how hard breathing was.

I began to think about trees.

I had a momentary nightmare that Batt was going to give us something as difficult to eat as hardshell crabs and steamed artichokes.

I leaned on Green-eye's shoulder and slept.

I think he slept too.

I woke when Batt lifted the cover from the stew pot. The odor pried my mouth open, reached down my throat, took hold of my stomach and twisted. I wasn't sure if it was pleasurable or painful. I just sat, working my jaws, my throat aching. I leaned forward over my knees and clutched sand.

Batt ladled stew into pans, stopping now and then to shake hair out of his eyes. I wondered how much hair was in the stew. I didn't care, mind you. Just curious. He passed the steaming tins and I rested mine in the hollow of my crossed legs. A charred loaf of bread came around. Knife broke open a piece and the fluffy innards popped through a gold streak on the crust. When I twisted some off, I realized the fatigue in my arms and shoulders and almost started laughing. I was too tired to eat, too hungry to sleep. With the paradox both sleeping and eating left the category of pleasure, where I'd always put them, and became duties on this crazy job I'd somehow got into. I sopped gravy on my bread, put it into my mouth, bit, and trembled.

I shoved down half my meal before I realized it was too

hot. Hungry like I was hungry, hungry beyond need—it's frightening to be that hungry.

Green-eye was shoving something into his mouth with his thumb.

That was the only other human thing I was aware of during the meal till Stinky spluttered, "Gimme some more!"

When I got my seconds, I managed to slow down enough to look around. You can tell about people from the way they eat. I remember the dinner Nativia had cooked us. Oh, eating were something else back then—a day ago, two days?

"You know," Batt grunted, watching his food go, "you got dessert coming."

"Where?" Knife answered, finishing his second helping and reaching out of the darkness for the bread.

"You have some more food-food first," Batt said, "'cause I'm damned if you're gonna eat up my dessert that fast." He leaned over, swiped Knife's pan from him, filled it, and those gray hands closed on the tin edge and withdrew into the shadow again. The sound of dogged chewing.

Spider, silent till now, looked with blinking silver eyes. "Good stew, cook."

Batt leered.

Spider who herds dragons; Spider who writes; Spider who has the multiplicated music of Kodaly in his head—good man to receive a compliment from.

I looked from Spider to Batt and back. I wished I had said *Good stew* because it was, and because saying it made Batt grin like that. What I did come out with, the words distorted by that incredible lash of hunger, was: "What's dessert?"

I guess Spider was a bigger person than me. Like I say, that sort of hunger is scary.

Batt took a ceramic dish out of the fire with rags. "Blackberry dumplings. Knife, reach me the rum sauce."

I heard Green-eye's breath change tempo. My mouth got wet all over again. I watched—examined Batt spooning dumplings and berry filling onto the pans.

"Knife, get your fingers out!"

". . . just wanted to taste." But the gray hand retreated. Through the dusk firelight caught on a tongue sliding along a lip.

Batt handed him a plate.

Spider was served last. We waited for him to begin, though, now that the bottom of the pit was lined.

"Night . . . sand . . . and dragons," Stinky muttered.

"Yeah." Which was very apt.

I had just taken my blade out to play when Spider said, "You were asking about Kid Death this morning."

"That's right." I lay the blade in my lap. "You had something to say about him?" The others quieted.

"I did the Kid a favor, once," Spider mused.

"When he was in the desert?" I asked, wondering what sort of person you would have to be to be different and doing Kid Death favors.

"When he had just come out of the desert," Spider said. "He was holed up in a town."

"What's a town?" I asked.

"You know what a village is?"

"Yeah. I came from one."

"And you know what a City is." He motioned around at the sand. "Well a village grows bigger and bigger till it becomes a town; then the town grows bigger and bigger till it becomes a City. But this was a ghost town. That means it was from a very old time, from the old people of the planet. It had stopped growing. The buildings had all broken open, sewers caved in, dead leaves fled up the streets, around the stubs of street-lamp bases; an abandoned power station, rats, snakes, department stores—these are the things that are in a town. Also the lowest, dirtiest outcasts of a dozen species who are vicious with a viciousness beyond what intelligence can conceive. Because if there were a brain behind it, they would all be luxuriant, decadent lords of evil over the whole world instead of wallowing in the junk heap of a ghost town. They are creatures you wouldn't put in a kage."

"What did you do for him?" I asked.

"Killed his father."

I frowned.

Spider picked at a tooth. "The Kid's dad was a detestable, three-eyed, three-hundred-pound worm. I know he'd murdered at least forty-six people. He tried to kill me three times while I was bumming through the town. Once with poison, once with a wrench, once with a grenade. Each time he missed and got somebody else. He'd fathered a couple of dozen, but still a good number less than he'd killed. Once, when I was on fair terms with him, he gave me one of his daughters. Butchered and dressed her himself. Fresh meat is scarce in town. He simply didn't count on one of his various kaged offspring whom he'd abandoned a thousand miles away following him up from the desert. Nor did he count on that child's being a criminal genius, psychotic, and a totally different creature. The Kid and I met up in town there where his father was living high as one could live in that dung pile. The Kid must have been about ten years old.

"I was sitting in a bar, listening to characters brag and boast, while a wrestling match was going in the corner. The loser would be dinner. Then this skinny carrottop wanders in and sits down on a pile of rags. He stared down most of the time so that you looked at those eyes of his through finer veils of gold. His skin was soap white. He watched the fight, listened to the bragging, and once made a design in the dirt with his toe. When the talk got boring, he scratched his elbow and made faces. When the stories got wild and fascinating, he froze, his fingers tied together, and head down. He listens like someone blind. When the stories were through, he walked out. Then someone whispered, *That was Kid Death!* and everybody got quiet. He already had quite a reputation."

Green-eye had moved a little closer to me. There was a chill over the City.

"A little later while I was taking a walk outside," Spider went on, "I saw him swimming in the lake of the Town Park.

Hey, Spiderman, he called me from the water.

I walked over and squatted by the pool's edge. *Hi, kid.*

You gotta kill my old man for me. He reached from the lake and grabbed my ankle. I tried to pull away. The Kid leaned back till his face was under water, and bubbled, *You gotta do me this little favor, Spider. You have to.*

A leaf stuck to his arm. *If you say so, Kid.*

He stood up in the water now, hair lank down his face, scrawny, white, and wet. *I say so.*

Mind if I ask why? I pushed the hair off his forehead. I wanted to see if he was real: cold fingers on my ankle; wet hair under my hand.

He smiled, ingenuous as a corpse. *I don't mind.* His lips, nipples, the cuticles over his claws were shriveled. *There's a whole lot of hate left on this world, Spiderman. The stronger you are, the more receptive you are to the memories that haunt these mountains, these rivers, seas, and jungles. And I'm strong! Oh, we're not human, Spider. Life and death, the real and the irrational aren't the same as they were for the poor race who willed us this world. They tell us young people, they even told me, that before our parents' parents came here, we were not concerned with love, life, matter, and motion. But we have taken a new home, and we have to exhaust the past before we can finish with the present. We have to live out the human if we are to move on to our own future. The past terrifies me. That's why I must kill it—why you must kill him for me.*

Are you so tied up with their past, Kid?

He nodded. *Untie me, Spider.*

What happens if I don't?

He shrugged. *I'll have to kill you—all.* He sighed. *Under the sea it's so silent . . . so silent, Spider.* He whispered, *Kill him!*

Where is he?

He's waddling along the street while the moonlit gnats make dust around his head, his heel sliding in the trickle of water along the gutter that runs from under the old church wall; he stops and leans, panting, against the moss—

He's dead, I said. I opened my eyes; *I dislodged a slab of concrete from the beams, so that it slid down—*

See you around sometime. The Kid grinned and pushed backward into the pool. *Thanks. Maybe I'll be able to do something for you someday, Spider.*

Maybe you will, I said. He sank in the silvered scum. I went back to the bar. They were roasting dinner."

After a while I said, "You must have lived in town a fair while."

"Longer than I'd like to admit," Spider said. "If you call it living." He sat up and glanced around the fire. "Lobey, Green-eye, you two circle the herd for the first watch. In three hours wake Knife and Stinky. Me and Batt will take the last shift."

Green-eye rose beside me. I stood too as the others made ready to sleep. My Mount was dozing. The moon was up. Ghost lights ran on the humped spines of the beasts. Sore-legged, stiff-armed, I climbed a-back My Mount and with Green-eye began to circle the herd. I swung the whip against my shin as we rode. "How do they look to you?"

I didn't expect an answer. But Green-eye rubbed his stomach with a grimy hand.

"Hungry? Yeah, I guess they are in all this sand." I watched the slender, dirty youngster sway behind the scaled hump. "Where are you from?" I asked.

He smiled quickly at me.

> *I was born of a lonely mother*
> *with neither father nor sister nor brother.*

I looked up surprised.

> *At the waters she waits for me*
> *my mother, my mother at Branning-at-sea.*

"You're from Branning-at-sea?" I asked.
He nodded.
"Then you're going home."
He nodded again.
Silent, we rode on till at last I began to play with tired fingers. Green-eye sang some more as we jogged under the moon.

I learned that his mother was a fine lady in Branning-at-sea, related to many important political leaders. He had been sent away with Spider to herd dragons for a year. He was returning at last to his mother, this year of wandering and work serving as some sort of passage rite. There was a great deal in the thin, bushy haired boy, so skilled with the flock, I didn't understand.

"Me?" I asked when his eye inquired of me in the last of the moonlight. "I don't have any time for the finery of Branning-at-sea as you describe it. I'll be glad to see it, passing. But I got things to do."

Silent inquiry.

"I'm going to Kid Death to get Friza, and stop what's killing all the different ones. That probably means stopping Kid Death."

He nodded.

"You don't know who Friza is," I said. "Why are you nodding?"

He cocked his head oddly, then looked across the herd.

I am different so I bring
words to singers when I sing.

I nodded and thought about Kid Death. "I hate him," I said. "I have to learn to hate him more so I can find him and kill him."

There is no death, only love.

That one arrived sideways.

"What was that again?"

He wouldn't repeat it. Which made me think about it more. He looked sadly out from the work-grime. At the horizon, the fat moon darkened with clouds. Strands of shadow through the thatch of his hair widened over the rest of his face. He blinked; he turned away. We finished our circuit, chased back two dragons. The moon, revealed once more, was a polished bone joint jammed on the sky. We woke Knife and Stinky, who rose and moved to their dragons.

The coals gave the only color. And for one moment when Green-eye crouched to stare at some pattern snaking the ashes, the light cast up on his single-eyed face. He stretched beside the fire.

I slept well, but a movement before dawn roused me. The moon was down. Starlight paled the sand. The coals were dead. One dragon hissed. Two moaned. Silence. Knife and Stinky were returning. Spider and Batt were getting up.

I drifted off and woke again when only one slop of blue lightened the eastern dunes. Batt's dragon came around the fireplace. Spider's lumbered after him. I rose on my elbows.

"Keeping you up?" Spider asked.

"Huh?"

"I was running over the Kodaly again."

"Oh." I could hear it coming across the chill sand. "Naw." I got to my feet. They were about to start around again. "Just a second. I'll go around with you. There's something I want to ask you. I'd have been up in a little while anyway."

He didn't wait, but I swung on my dragon and caught up.

He laughed softly when I reached his side. "Wait till you've been out here a few more days. You won't be so ready to give up that last few minutes' sleep."

"I'm too sore to sleep," I said, though the jogging was beginning to loosen stiff me. The coolness had set my joints. "What did you want to ask me?"

"About Kid Death."

"What about him?"

"You say you knew him. Where can I find him?"

Spider was silent. My Mount slipped in the road and caught his balance again before he answered. "Even if I could tell, even if telling you would do any good, why should I? The Kid could get rid of you like that." He popped his whip on the sand. Grains flew. "I don't think the Kid would appreciate my going around telling people who want to kill him where to find him."

"I don't suppose it would make much difference if he's as strong as you say he is." I ran my thumb over the machete's mouthpiece.

Spider shrugged some of his shoulders. "Maybe not. But, like I say, the Kid's my friend."

"Got you under his thumb too, huh?" It's difficult to be cutting with a cliché. I tried.

"Just about," Spider said.

I flicked my whip at a dragon who looked like he was thinking of leaving. He yawned, shook his mane, and lay back down. "I guess in a way he's even got me. He said I would try to find him until I had learned enough. Then I'd try to run away."

"He's playing with you," Spider said. He had a mocking smile.

"He's really got us all tied up."

"Just about," Spider said again.

I frowned. "Just about isn't all."

"Well," Spider said in some other direction than mine, "there are a few he can't touch, like his father. That's why he had to get me to kill him."

"Who?"

"Green-eye is one. Green-eye's mother is another."

"Green-eye?" In my repetition of the name I'd asked a question. Perhaps he didn't hear. Perhaps he chose not to answer.

So I asked another. "Why did Green-eye have to leave Branning-at-sea? He half explained to me last night, but didn't quite get it."

"He has no father," Spider said. He seemed more ready to talk of this.

"Can't they run a paternity check? The traveling folk-doctors do it all the time in my village."

"I didn't say they didn't know who his father was. I said he had none."

I frowned.

"How are your genetics?"

"I can draw a dominance chart with the best of them," I said. Most people, even from the tiniest villages, knew their genetics, even if they couldn't add. The human chromosome system was so inefficient in the face of the radiation level that genetics was survival knowledge. I've often wondered why we didn't invent a more compatible method of reproduction to go along with our own three way I-guess-you'd-call-it-sexual devision. Just lazy. "Go on," I said to Spider.

"Green-eye had no father," Spider repeated.

"Parthenogenesis?" I asked. "That's impossible. The sex distinguishing chromosome is carried by the male. Females and androgynes only carry genetic equipment for producing other females. He'd have to be a girl, with haploid chromosomes, and sterile. And he certainly isn't a girl." I thought a moment. "Of course if he were a bird, it would be a different matter. The females carry the sex distinguishing chromosomes there." I looked out over the herd. "Or a lizard."

"But he's not," Spider said.

I agreed. "That's amazing," I said, looking back towards the fire where the amazing boy slept.

Spider nodded. "When he was born, wise men came from all over to examine him. He is haploid. But he's quite potent and quite male, though a rather harried life has made him chaste by temperament."

"Too bad."

Spider nodded. "If he would join actively in the solstice orgies or make some appeasing gesture in the autumnal harvest celebrations, a good deal of the trouble could be avoided."

I raised an eyebrow. "Who's to know if he takes part in the orgies? Don't you hold them in the dark of the moon in Branning?"

Spider laughed. "Yes. But at Banning-at-sea, it's become a rather formal business; it's carried on with artificial insemination. The presentation of the seed—especially by the men of important families—gets quite a bit of publicity."

"Sounds very dry and impersonal."

"It is. But efficient. When a town has more than a million people in it, you can't just turn out the lights and let everybody run wild in the streets the way you can in a small village. They tried it that way a couple of times, back when Branning-at-sea was much smaller, and even then the results were—"

"A million people?" I said. "There are a million people in Branning-at-sea?"

"Last census there were three million six hundred fifty thousand."

I whistled. "That's a lot."

"That's more than you can imagine."

I looked across the herd of dragons; only a couple of hundred.

"Who wants to take part in an orgy of artificial insemination?" I asked.

"In a larger society," Spider said, "things have to be carried out that way. Until there's a general balancing of the genetic reservoir, the only thing to do is to keep the genes mixing, mixing, mixing. But we have become clannish, more so in places like Branning-at-sea than in the hills. How to keep people from having no more than one child by the same partner. In a backwoods settlement, a few nights of license take care of it, pretty much. In Branning, things have to be assured by mathematical computation. And families have sprung up that would be quite glad to start doubling their children if given half a chance. Anyway, Green-eye just goes about his own business, occasionally saying very upsetting things to the wrong person. The fact that he's different and immune to Kid Death, from a respected family, and rather chary of ritual observances makes him quite controversial. Everybody blames the business on his parthenogenetic birth."

"They frown on that even where I come from," I told Spider. "It means his genetic structure is identical with his mother's. That will never do. If that happens enough, we shall all return to the great rock and the great roll in no time."

"You sound like one of those pompous fools at Branning." He was annoyed.

"Huh! That's just what I've been taught."

"Think a little more. Every time you say that, you bring Green-eye a little closer to death."

"What?"

"They've tried to kill him before. Why do you think he was sent away?"

"Oh," I said. "Then why is he coming back?"

"He wants to." Spider shrugged. "Can't very well stop him if he wants to."

I grunted. "You don't make Branning-at-sea sound like a very nice place. Too many people, half of them crazy, and they don't even know how to have an orgy." I took up my blade. "I don't have time for nonsense like that."

The music dirged from Spider. I played light piping sounds.

"Lobey."

I looked back at him.

"Something's happening, Lobey, something now that's happened before, before when the others were here. Many of us are worried about it. We have the stories about what went on, what resulted when it happened to the others. It may be very serious. All of us may be hurt."

"I'm tired of the old stories," I said, "their stories. We're not them; we're new, new to this world, this life. I know the stories of Lo Orpheus and Lo Ringo. Those are the only ones I care about. I've got to find Friza."

"Lobey—"

"This other is no concern of mine." I let a shrill note. "Wake your herders, Spider. You have dragons to drive."

I galloped My Mount forward. Spider didn't call again.

Before the sun hit apogee the edge of the City cleft the horizon. As I swung my whip in the failing heat, I permutated Green-eye's last words, beating out thoughts in time: if there were no death, how might I gain Friza? That love was enough, if wise and articulate and daring. Or thinking of La

Dire, who would have amended it (dragons clawed from the warm sand to the leafy hills), there is no death, only rhythm. When the sand reddened behind us, and the foundering beasts, with firmer footing, hastened, I took out my knife and played.

The City was behind us.

Dragons loped, easy now across the gorse. A stream ribboned the knolly land and the beasts stopped to slosh their heads in the water, scraping their hind feet on the bank, through grass, through sand, to black soil. The water lapped their knees, grew muddy as they tore the water-weeds. A fly bobbed on a branch, preening the crushed prism of his wing (a wing the size of my foot) and thought a linear, arthropod music. I played it for him, and he turned the red bowl of his eye to me and whispered wondering praise. Dragons threw back their heads, gargling.

There is no death.

Only music.

Whanne, as he strod alonge the shakeynge lee,
The roddie levynne glesterrd on hys headde;
Into hys hearte the azure vapoures spreade;
He wrythde arounde yn drearie dernie payne;—
Whanne from his lyfe-bloode the rodde lemes were fed,
He felle an hepe of ashes on the playne.

Thomas Chatterton, "English Metamorphosis"

"Now there's a quaint taste," said Durcet. "Well, Curval, what do you think of that one?"

"Marvelous," the President replied; "there you have an individual who wishes to make himself familiar with the idea of death and hence unafraid of it, and who to that end has found no better means than to associate it with a libertine idea . . ." . . . Supper was served, orgies followed as usual, the household retired to bed.

Le Marquis de Sade, *The 120 Days of Sodom*

The motion of gathering loops of water
Must either burst or remain in a moment.
The violet colors through the glass
Throw up little swellings that appear
And spatter as soon as another strikes
And is born; so pure are they of colored
Hues, that we feel the absent strength
Of its power. When they begin they gather
Like sand on the beach: each bubble
Contains a complete eye of water.

Samuel Greenberg, "The Glass Bubbles"

Then to the broken land ("This"—Spider halted his dragon in the shaly afternoon—"is the broken land." He flung a small flint over the edge. It chuckled into the canyon. Around us the dragons were craning curiously at the granite, the veined cliffs, the chasms) slowing our pace now. Clouds dulled the sun. Hot fog flowed around the rocks. I worked one muscle after another against the bone to squeeze out the soreness. Most of the pain (surprise) was gone. We meandered through the fabulous, simple stones.

The dragons made half time here.

Spider said it was perhaps forty kilometers to Branning-at-sea. Wind heated our faces. Glass wound in the rocks. Five dragons began a scuffle on the shale. One was the tumored female. Green-eye and me came at them from opposite sides. Spider was busy at the head of the herd; the scuffle was near the tail. Something had frightened them, and they were plopping up the slope. It didn't occur to us something was wrong; this was the sort of thing that Spider (and Friza) were supposed to be able to prevent. (Oh, Friza, I'll find you through the echo of all mourning stones, all praising trees!) We followed.

They dodged through the boulders. I shouted after them. Our whips chattered. We couldn't outrun them. We hoped they would fall to fighting again. We lost them for a minute, then heard their hissing beyond the rocks, lower down.

Clouds smeared the sky; water varnished the trail ahead. As M. M. crossed the wet rock, he slipped.

I was thrown, scraping hip and shoulder. I heard my blade clatter away on the rock. My whip snarled around my neck. For one moment I thought I'd strangle. I rolled down a slope, trying to flail myself to a halt, got scraped up more. Then I dropped over the edge of something. I grabbed out with both hands and feet. Chest and stomach slapped stone. My breath went off somewhere and wouldn't go back into my lungs for a long time. When it did, it came roaring down my sucking throat, whirled in my bruised chest. Busted ribs? Just pain.

And roar again with another breath. Tears flooded my sight.

I was holding on to a rock with my left hand, a vine with my right; my left foot clutched a sapling none too securely by the roots. My right leg dangled. And I just knew it was a long way down.

I rubbed my eye on my shoulder and looked up:

The lip of the trail above me.

Above that, angry sky.

Sound? Wind through gorse somewhere. No music.

While I was looking it started to rain. Sometimes painful catastrophes happen. Then some little or even pleasant thing follows it, and you cry. Like rain. I cried.

"Lobey."

I looked again.

Kneeling on a shelf of stone a few feet above me to the right was Kid Death.

"Kid—?"

"Lobey," he said, shaking wet hair back from his forehead. "I judge you can hold on there twenty-seven minutes before you drop over the edge from exhaustion. So I'm going to wait twenty-six minutes before I do anything about saving your life. O.K.?"

I coughed.

Seeing him close, I guessed he was sixteen or seventeen, or maybe a baby-faced twenty. His skin was wrinkled at his wrists, neck, and under his arms.

Rain kept dribbling in my eyes; my palms stung, and what I was holding on to was getting slippery.

"Ever run into any good westerns?" He shook his head. "Too bad. Nothing I like better than westerns." He rubbed his forefinger under his nose and sniffed. Rain danced on his shoulders as he leaned over to talk to me.

"What is a 'western'?" I asked. My chest still hurt. "And you mean you're really going to make—" I coughed again "—me hang here twenty-six minutes?"

"It's an art-form the Old Race, the humans, had before we came," Kid Death said. "And yes, I am. Torture is an art-form too. I want to rescue you at the last minute. While I'm waiting,

I want to show you something." He pointed up to the rim of the road I'd rolled over.

Friza looked down.

I stopped breathing. The pain in my chest exploded, my wide eyes burned with rain. Dark face, slim wet shoulders, then watch her turn her head (gravel sliding under my belly, the whiplash still around my neck and the handle swinging against my thigh) to catch rain in her mouth. She looked back, and I saw (or did I hear?) her wonder at life returned, and confusion at the rain, these twisted rocks, these clouds. Glory beat behind those eyes above me. Articulate, she would have called my name; saw me, now, impulsively reached her hand to me (did I hear her fear?).

"Friza!"

That was a scream.

You and I know the word I shrieked. But nobody else hearing the rough sound my lungs shoved up would have recognized it.

All this, understand, in the instant it takes to open your eyes in the rain, lick a drop from your lip, then focus on what's in front of you and realize it's somebody you love about to die and he tries to scream your name. That's what Friza did there on the road's lip.

And I kept screaming.

What Kid Death did between us was giggle.

Friza began to search right and left for a way to get down to me. She rose, disappeared, was back a moment later, bending a sapling over the edge of the road.

"No, Friza!"

But she started to climb down, dirt and tiny stones shooting out beneath her feet. Then, when she was hanging at the very end, the line of her body arching dark on the rock, she grabbed the whip handle—neither with hands nor feet, but rather as she had once thrown a pebble, as Spider had once pushed over a chunk of cement; she grabbed the handle from where it hung against my thigh, pulled it, lifted it, straining till rain glistened on her sides, knotted the handle around the sapling above the first fork. She started to climb back, jerk of an arm, away a moment, jerk, away, jerk, reaching handhold by handhold towards the road. It kept on going through my head, here she wakes from how many days' death with only a moment to glory before plunging into the rescue of the life running out below her. She was doing it to save me. She wanted me to grab hold of the whip and haul myself to the tree, then by the tree haul myself to the road. I hurt and loved her, held on and didn't fall.

Kid Death was still chuckling. Then he pointed at the apex of the bent tree. "Break!" he whispered.

It did.

She fell, throwing the branch away from her in one instant; clutching at the stone as she fell, snatched at the length of leather dangling from my neck, then let it go.

She let it go because she knew damn well it would have pulled me from the cliff face.

"Baaa—baaa!" Kid Death said. He was imitating a ewe. Then he giggled again.

I slammed my face against the shale. *"Friza!"* No, you couldn't understand what I howled.

Her music crashed out with her brains on the rocks of the canyon floor a hundred feet below.

Rock. Stone. I tried to become the rock I hung against. I tried to be stone. Less blasted by her double death I would have dropped. Had she died in any other act than trying to save me, I would have died with her. But I couldn't let her fail.

My heart rocked. My heart rolled.

Numb, I dangled for some timeless time, till my hands began to slip.

"All right. Up you go."

Something seized my wrist and pulled me up, hard. My shoulders rang like gongs of pain under my ears. I was hauled blind over gravel. I blinked and breathed. Somehow Kid Death had pulled me up on the ledge with him.

"Just saved your life," Kid Death said. "Aren't you glad you know me?"

I began to shake. I was going to pass out.

"You're just about to yell at me, 'You killed her!'" Kid Death said. "I killed her again is what really happened. And I may have to do it a third time before you get the idea—"

I lunged, would have gone off and over. But he caught me with one strong, wet hand, and slapped me with the other. The rain had stopped.

Maybe he did more than slap me.

The Kid turned and started scrambling up to the lip of the trail. I started after him.

I climbed.

Dirt ripped under my fingers. It's good about my nail chewing, because otherwise I wouldn't have had any nails left. From the ledge it was possible to get back up. Kid Death leaped and bounded. I crawled.

There's a condition where every action dogs one end. You move/breathe/stop to rest/start again with one thing in mind. That's how I followed. Mostly on my belly. Mostly with my breath held. I'm not too sure where I went. Things didn't clear up till I realized there were two figures in front of me: the moist, white redhead. A black thatch of hair, grimy Green-eye.

I lay on a rock, resting, is how it was, in the fog of fatigue and endeavor, when I saw them.

Kid Death stood with his arm around Green-eye's shoulder at the precipice. The sky in front of them swam violently.

"Look, pardner," Kid Death was saying; "we've got to come to some sort of agreement. I mean, you don't think I came all the way out here just to rustle five dragons from my friend Spider? That's just to let him know I'm still in the running. But you. You and I have to get together. Haploid? You're totally outside my range. I want you. I want you very much, Green-eye."

The dirty herder shrugged from under the moist fingers.

"Look," Kid Death said and gestured at the crazy sky.

As I had first seen the Kid's face in the glittering screen in the source-cave, I saw in the raveling clouds: a plain surrounded by a wire fence (a kage?) but inside a soaring needle wracked with struts and supports. I got some idea how big it was when I realized the stone blocks by the fence were houses, and the dots moving around were men and women.

"Starprobe," the Kid said. "They're on the verge of discovering the method the humans used to get from planet to planet, star to star. They've been delving in the ruins, tasting the old ideas, licking the bits of metal and wire now for ten years. It's almost finished." He waved his hand. Rolling in place of the scene now was water and water: an ocean. On the water, metal pontoons formed a floating station. Boats plied back and forth. Cranes dropped a metal cabinet towards the ocean floor. "Depthgauge," the Kid explained. "Soon we shall be able to do more than dream across the silt of the ocean floor, but take these bodies to the fond of the world as they did." Another wave of the hand and we were looking underground. Segmented worms, driven by women with helmets. "Rockdrill, going on now in the place they called Chile." Then, at a final motion, we were looking at myriad peoples all involved in labor, grinding grain, or toiling with instruments gleaming and baffling and complex. "There," said Kid Death, "there are the deeds and doings of all the men and women and androgynes on this world to remember the wisdom of the old ones. I can hand you the wealth produced by the hands of them all." (Green-eye's green eye widened.) "I can guarantee it. You know I can. All you have to do is join me."

The white hand had landed on Green-eye's shoulder. Again he shrugged from under it.

"What power do you have?" Kid Death demanded. "What can you do with your difference! Speak to a few deaf men, dead men, pierce the minds of a few idiots?" I suddenly realized the Kid was very upset. And he wanted Green-eye to agree with him.

Green-eye started to walk away.

"Hey, Green-eye!" Kid Death bellowed. I saw his stomach sink as the air emptied from his chest. His claws knotted.

Green-eye glanced back.

"That rock!" The Kid motioned towards a chunk at the cliff's edge. "Turn that there rock into something to eat."

Green-eye rubbed his dirty finger behind his ear.

"You've been on this dragon drive now twenty-seven days. You've been away from Branning-at-sea a few days short of a year. Turn that log into a bed, like you used to sleep in at your mother's palace. You're a Prince at Branning-at-sea and you smell like lizard droppings. That puddle, make it an onyx bath with water any one of five temperatures controlled by a lever with a copper rat's head on the tip. You've got callouses on your palms and your legs are bowing from straddling a dragon's hump. Where are the dancers who danced for you on the jade tiles of the terrace? Where are the musicians who eased the evenings? Turn this mountain-top into a place worthy of you—"

I think this is when Green-eye looked up and saw me. He started for me, only stopped to pick up my machete that was lying at the foot of the rock, then vaulted up beside me.

On the cliff edge the Kid had gotten furious. He quivered, teeth meshed tight, fists balled against his groin. Suddenly, he whirled and cried something—

Thunder.

It shocked me and I jerked back. Green-eye ignored it and tried to help me sit up. At the cliff's edge, Kid Death shook his arms. Lightning flared down the clouds. The leaves bleached from black to lavender. Green-eye didn't even blink. Thunder again; then someone flung buckets of water.

Herder dirt turned to mud on Green-eye's shoulder as he helped me down the slope. Something wasn't right inside me. Things kept going out inside me. The rain was cold. I was shivering. Somehow it was easier just to relax, not to hold on . . .

Green-eye was shaking my shoulder. I opened my eyes to the rain, and the first thing I did was reach out for my blade. Green-eye held it out of reach; he was glaring at me.

"Huh . . . ? Wha . . ." My fingers and toes tingled. "What happened?" Rain stung my ears, my lips.

Green-eye was crying, his lips snarling back from his white teeth. Rain streaked the dirt on his face, sleeked down his hair; he kept shaking my shoulder, desolate and furious.

"What happened?" I asked. "Did I pass out . . . ?"

You died! He stared at me, unbelievingly, angry, and streaming. *God damn it, Lobey! Why did you have to die! You just gave up; you just decided it wasn't worth it, and you let the heart stop and the brain blank! You died, Lobey! You died!*

"But I'm not dead now . . ."

No. He helped me forward. *The music's going on again. Come on.*

Once more I reached for my blade. He let me have it. There was nothing to hack at. I just felt better holding it. It was raining too hard to play.

We found our mounts moaning in the torrent and flinging their whiskers around happily. Green-eye helped me up. Astride a wet dragon, saddle or no, is as difficult as riding a greasy earthquake. We finally found the herd up ahead, moving slowly through the downpour.

Spider rode up to us. "There you are! I thought we'd lost you! Get over to the other side and keep them out of the prickly pears. Makes them drunk and you can't handle them."

So we rode over to the other side and kept them out of the prickly pears. I kept phrasing sentences in my head to tell Spider about what happened. I chewed over the words, but I couldn't gnaw them into sense. Once, when the pressure of disbelief grew so large I couldn't hold it, I reined my dragon around and dashed across the muddy slope towards Spider. "Boss, Kid Death is riding with—"

I'd make a mistake. The figure who turned wasn't Spider. Above shriveled lids and scrotum red hair slicked white brow and belly. Needle teeth snagged the thunder that erupted from behind the mountains as he threw back his head in doomed laughter. Naked on his dragon, he waved a black and silver hat over his head. Two ancient guns hung holstered at his hips, with milky handles glimmering. As his dragon reared (and mine danced back) I saw, strapped to his bare, clawed feet, a set of metal cages with revolving barbs that he heeled into his beast's flank, cruelly as a flower.

Dazed, I punched rain from my eyes. But the illusion (with veined temples gleaming with rain) was gone. Gagging on wonder, I rode back to the rim of the herd.

It is in the lightning and the thunder of the elements
that warm him so that he takes time to pause and to re-
flect. There is a dragon there. They do not hear, nor
does he. The elements have rendered voice inaudible.
There is a dragon there.

Hunce Voelker, *The Hart Crane Voyages*

It is not that love sometimes makes mistakes, but that it
is, essentially, a mistake. We fall in love when our imagi-
nation projects nonexistent perfections on to another
person. One day the phantasmagoria vanishes, and with
it love dies.

Ortega y Gasset, *On Love*

Exhaustion numbed me; routine kaged me. It had stopped
raining almost an hour before I realized it. And the land had
changed.

We had left the rocks. Wet shrubs and briars fell before the
dragons' claws. To our left, a strip of gray ground ran along
with us, just down a small slope. Once I asked Stinky, "Are we
following that funny strip of stone down there?"

He chuckled and sputtered, "Hey, Lobey, that's the first
paved road I bet you ever seen. Right?"

"I guess so," I said. "What's *paved?*"

Knife, who was riding by, snickered. Stinky went off to do
something else. That was the last I heard of it. Three or four
carts trundled by on the road before it struck me what the
damn thing was used for. Very clever. When the next one
came by, I remembered to stare. It was late afternoon. I was
so tired all the world's wonders might have bounced on the
balls of my eyes without leaving a picture.

Most of the carts were pulled by four- or six-legged animals that I was vaguely familiar with. But new animals are not strange sights when your own flock might lamb any monster. One cart made me start, though.

It was low, of black metal, and had no beast at all before or behind. It purred along the road ten times the speed of the others and was gone in smoke before I had time to really see it. A few dragons who had ignored the other vehicles shied now and hissed. Spider called to me as I stared after it, "Just one of the wonders of Branning-at-sea."

I turned back to calm the offended lizards.

The next time I glanced at the road I saw the picture. It was painted on a large stand mounted by the pavement, so that all who passed could see. It was the face of a young woman with cotton white hair, a childish smile, her shoulders shrugged. She had a small chin, and green eyes that looked widened by some pleasant surprise. Her lips were slightly opened over small, shadowed teeth.

THE DOVE SAYS, "ONE IS *nice?* NINE OR TEN ARE SO MUCH *nicer!*"

I spelled out the caption and frowned. Batt was within hollering distance so I hollered. "Hey, who's that?"

"The *Dove!*" he howled, shaking the hair back from his shoulders. "He wants to know who the Dove is!" and the rest of them laughed too. As we got closer and closer to Branning-at-sea I became the butt of more and more jokes. I stuck closer to Green-eye; he didn't make fun of me. The first evening wind blew on the small of my back, the back of my neck and dried the sweat before more sweat rolled. I was staring dutifully at dragon scales when Green-eye stopped and pointed ahead. I looked up. Or rather down.

We had just crested a hill, and the land sloped clear and away to—well, if it were twenty meters away it was a great toy. If it were twenty kilometers away it was just great. Paved roads joined in that white and aluminum confusion at the purple water. Someone had started building it, and it had gotten out of hand and started building itself. There were grand squares where cactuses and palms grew and swayed; occasional hills where trees and lawns ranged about single buildings; many sections of tiny houses shoved and jammed on twisting streets. Beyond, from glazed docks ships plied the watery evening through its harbors.

"Branning-at-sea," Spider said, beside me. "That's it."

I blinked. The sun laid our shadows forward, warmed our necks, and blazed in the high windows. "It's large," I said.

"Right down there"—Spider pointed; I couldn't follow because there was so much to look at, so I listened—"is where we take the herd. This whole side of Branning lives off the herding business. The seaside survives through fishing and trade with the islands."

The others gathered around us. Familiar with the magnificence and squalor below, they grew silent as we went down.

We passed another signboard by the road. This time the Dove was shown from another angle, winking through the twilight.

THE DOVE SAYS, "THOUGH TEN ARE NICE, NINETY-NINE OR A HUNDRED ARE *SO* MUCH NICER!"

As I looked, lights came on above the twenty-foot-high face. The huge, insouciant expression leaped at us. I must have looked surprised because Spider thumbed towards it and said, "They keep it lighted all night so passersby can read what the Dove has to say." He smiled as though he were telling me something slightly off-color. Now he coiled his whip. "We'll camp down on the plateau there for the evening and go into Branning at dawn." Twenty minutes later we were circling the herd while Batt fixed dinner. The sky was black beyond the ocean, blue overhead. Branning cast up lights of its own, sparkling like sequins fallen on the shore. Perhaps it was the less violent terrain, perhaps it was Spider's calm, but the dragons were perfectly still.

Afterward, I lay down, but didn't sleep. Along with Knife I had mid-watch. When Green-eye shook my shoulder with his foot, I rolled to standing; anticipatory excitement kept me awake. I would leave the herders; where would I go next?

Knife and I circled the herd in opposite directions. As I rode I reflected: to be turned loose by my lonesome in the woods is a fairly comfortable situation. Turned loose among stone, glass, and a few million people is something else. Four-fifths of the herd slept. A few moaned towards Branning, less bright than before, still a sieve of light on the sea. I reined my mount to gaze at the—

"Hey up there, Dragonman!"

I looked down the bank.

A hunchback had stopped his dog cart on the road.

"Hi down there."

"Taking your lizards into Branning at dawn?" He grinned, then dug beneath the leather flap over the cart and pulled out a melon. "You hungry, herder?" He broke it open and made to hurl me half.

But I slung down from my mount and he held. I scrambled to the road. "Hey, thank you Lo stranger."

He laughed. "No Lo for me."

Just then the dog, looking back and forth between the man and me, began to whine. "Me. Me. Me hungry Me."

The hunchback handed me my half, then ruffled the dog's ears. "You had your dinner."

"I'll share mine," I said.

The hunchback shook his head. "He works for me and I feed him."

He broke apart his piece and tossed the piece to the animal, who drove his snout into it, champing. As I bit into my melon, the stranger asked me, "Where are you from, Dragonman?"

I gave him the name of my village.

"And this is your first time to Branning-at-sea?"

"It is. How could you tell?"

"Oh." He grinned over a crowd of yellow teeth. "I came to Branning-at-sea a first time myself. There are a few things that set you off from the natives down there, a couple of points that make you different—"

"Different?"

He raised his hand. "No offense meant."

"None taken."

The hunchback chuckled once more as I took a sweet wet mouthful.

"What's diamond here is dung there," he pronounced sagely. "No doubt the Dove said that at one time or another."

"The Dove," I said. "She's La Dove, isn't she?"

He looked surprised. "The Lo, La, and Le is confusing here. No." He scraped the rind with his front teeth and spun it away. "Diamond and dung. I gather it worked in your town like it did in mine. Lo and La and Le titles reserved for potent normals and eventually bestowed on potent functionals?"

"That's the way it is."

"Was. It was that way in Branning-at-sea. It's not the way it is now. So little is known about difference in the villages that nobody gets angry at being called such."

"But I am different," I said. "Why should I be angry? That's the way it is."

"Again, that's the way it was in Branning. Not the way it is now. A third time: diamond and dung. I just hope your backwoods ways don't get you into trouble. Mine got me half a dozen thrashings when I first got to Branning-at-sea, fifteen years ago. And even then the place was much smaller than it is now." He looked down the road.

I recalled what Spider had said about titling herders. "How does it work now?" I asked. "I mean here? At Branning-at-sea?"

"Well"—the hunchback hooked his thumbs under his belt—"there are about five families that control everything that goes on in Branning-at-sea, own all the ships, take in rent on half the houses, will probably pay your salary and buy up those dragons. They, along with fifteen or twenty celebrities, like the Dove, take Lo or La when you address them in person. But you'll find some pretty non-functional people with those titles."

"Well, how am I to know them then, if their obvious functionality doesn't matter?"

"You'll know them if you run into them—but it's not very

likely you will. You can spend a lifetime at Branning-at-sea and never have to Lo or La once. But if you go about titling everyone you meet, or bridling when someone doesn't use a title to you, you'll be taken for a fool, or crazy, or at best recognized as a village lout."

"I'm not ashamed of my village!"

He shrugged. "I didn't suggest you were. Only trying to answer your questions."

"Yes. I understand. But what about difference?"

The hunchback put his tongue in his cheek, then took it out. "At Branning-at-sea difference is a private matter. Difference is the foundation of those buildings, the pilings beneath the docks, tangled in the roots of the trees. Half the place was built on it. The other half couldn't live without it. But to talk about it in public reveals you to be ill-mannered and vulgar."

"They talk about it." I pointed back to the herd. "I mean the other dragon drivers."

"And they are vulgar. Now if you hang with herders all the time—and you can spend your life that way if you want—you can talk about it all you want."

"But I *am* different—" I began again.

Having told me once, his patience with me and the subject ended.

"—but I guess I better keep it to myself," I finished.

"Not a bad idea." He spoke sternly.

But how could I tell him about Friza? How could I search if our differences were secret? "You," I said after embarrassed silence. "What do you do at Branning-at-sea?"

The question pleased him. "Oh, I run a little meeting place where the tired can sit, the hungry can eat, the thirsty can drink, and the bored can find entertainment." He ended his pronouncement by flinging his red cape back over his misshapen shoulder.

"I'll come and visit you," I said.

"Well," mused the hunchback, "not many herders come to my place; it's a bit refined. But after you've been in Branning-at-sea for a while and you think you can behave yourself, come around with some silver in your wallet. Though I'll take most of it away from you, you'll have a good time."

"I'll be sure to come," I said. I was thinking of Kid Death. I was journeying down the long night. I was searching out Friza. "What's your name and where can I find you?"

"My name is Pistol, but you can forget that. You'll find me at *The Pearl*—the name of my place of business."

"It sounds fascinating."

"The most fascinating thing the likes of you have ever seen," he said modestly.

"Can't pass that up. What are you doing out on the paved road this late?"

"Same as yourself, going to Branning-at-sea."

"Where are you coming from?"

"My outland friend, your manners are incredible. Since you ask, I come from friends who live outside Branning. I brought them gifts; they gave me gifts in return. But since they are not friends of yours, you shouldn't inquire after them."

"I'm sorry." I felt slightly rankled at this formality I didn't understand.

"You don't understand all this, do you?" He softened a little. "But when you've worn shoes a while and kept your navel covered, it will make more sense. I tell you all this now, but a year in Branning-at-sea will jack up my jabber with meaning."

"I don't intend to stay a year."

"You may not. Then, you may stay the rest of your life. It's that sort of place. It holds many wonders and its wonders may hold you."

"I'm passing," I insisted. "The death of Kid Death is at the end of my trip."

He got the oddest look. "I tell you, woodsboy," he admonished, "forget rough herders' talk. Don't swear by nightmares to your betters."

"I'm not swearing. The redheaded pest rides with this herd to plague Green-eye and me."

Hunched Pistol decided that the oaf (who was me) was beyond tutoring. He laughed and clapped my shoulder. That vulgar streak in him that had first prompted him to open conversation came out again. "Then good luck to you, Lo Dirty-face and may the different devil die soon and by your hand."

"By my knife," I corrected, drawing my machete for him to see. "Think of a song."

"What?"

"Think of some song. What music do they play at your pearl?"

He frowned, and I played.

His eyes widened, then he laughed. He leaned against his wagon, slapped his stomach. The thing inside me that laughs or cries laughed with him awhile. I played. But when his humor was past my understanding, I sheathed my machete.

"Dragon driver," he explained through his laughter, "I have only two choices, to mock your ignorance, or assume that you mock me."

"As you said to me, no offense meant. But I wish you'd explain the joke."

"I have, several times. You persist." He examined my puzzlement. "Keep your differences to *yourself*. They are your affair, nobody else's."

"But it's only music."

"Friend, what would you think of a man you just met who, three minutes into the conversation, announced the depth of his navel?"

"I don't see the point."

He beat his forehead with his fingers. "I must remember my own origins. Once I was as ignorant as you; I swear, though, I can't remember when." He pendulumed between humor and exasperation faster than I followed.

"Look," I said. "I don't see the pattern in your formality. What I do see I don't like—"

"It's not for you to judge," Pistol said. "You can accept it, or you can go away. But you can't go around disregarding other people's customs, joking with the profane, and flaunting the damned."

"Will you *please* tell me what customs I've disregarded, what I've flaunted? I've just said what was on my mind."

His country face hardened again (hard country faces I was to become used to in Branning). "You talk about Lo Green-eye as if he rode by you among the lizards and you hail Kid Death as though you yourself have looked down his six-gun."

"And where"—I was angry—"do you think Green-eye is? He's sleeping by the coals up there." I pointed up the rise. "And Kid Death—"

Fire surprised us and we whirled. Behind us in flame, he stood up and smiled. As he pushed back the brim of his hat with the barrel of his gun, red hair fell. "Howdy, pardners," he snickered. Shadow from grass and rock jogged on the ground. Where flame slapped his wet skin, steam curled away.

"Ahhhhhh-ahhhh—*ahhhh*-eeeeee!" That was Pistol. He fell against his cart, his jaw flopped down. He closed it to swallow, but it fell open again. The dog growled. I stared.

The fire flared, flickered, dimmed. Then only the smell of leaves. My eyes pulsed with the afterimage and rage. I looked around me. Pulsing darkness moved with my eyes. Behind it, on the rise by the road, the light from the road lamp brushing his knees, was Green-eye. He rubbed the tiredness out of his face with his fist. Kid Death had gone to wherever he goes.

The cart started behind me.

Pistol was still trying to get seated and at the same time guide the dog. I thought he was going to fall. He didn't. They trundled away. I climbed up to Green-eye's side. He looked at me . . . sadly?

In the light up from the road, his sharp cheekbones were only slightly softened by wisps of adolescent beard. His shadowed socket was huge.

We went back to the fire. I lay down. Sleep pawed my eyes down and the balls beneath my lids exploded till dawn with amazing dreams of Friza.

The Dove has torn her wing so no more songs of love.
We are not here to sing: we're here to kill the Dove.

Jacques Brel, "*La Colombe*"

Jean Harlow? Christ, Orpheus, Billy the Kid, those three
I can understand. But what's a young spade writer like
you doing all caught up with the Great White Bitch?!
Of course I guess it's pretty obvious.

Gregory Corso, *In conversation*

I
think of people *sighing* over poetry, *using* it,
I
    don't know what it's for . . .
"Oh, I'll give your bores back!"

Joanne Kyger, "The Pigs for Circe in May"

She is with me evenings.
    My ear is funnel for all voice and trill and warble you can
conceive this day.
    She is with me mornings.

Came back to the house early. They have brought wine for New Year. There were musicians down in the white city. I remember a year and a half ago when I finished *The Fall of The Towers*, saying to myself, you are twenty-one years old, going on twenty-two: you are too old to get by as a child prodigy: your accomplishments are more important than the age at which they were done; still, the images of youth plague me, Chatterton, Greenberg, Radiguet. By the end of TEI I hope to have excised them. Billy the Kid is the last to go. He staggers through this abstracted novel like one of the mad children in Crete's hills. Lobey will hunt you down, Billy. Tomorrow, weather permitting, I will return to Delos to explore the ruins around the Throne of Death in the center of the island that faces the necropolis across the water on Rhenia.

Writer's Journal, Mykonos, December 1965

Throughout most of the history of man the importance of ritual has been clearly recognized, for it is through the ritual acts that man establishes his identity with the restorative powers of nature or makes and helps effect his passage into higher stages of personal development and experience.

Masters & Houston, *The Varieties of Psychedelic Experience*

The lights of Branning were yellow behind mist and brambles as, through the chill, night made its blue, wounded retreat. Sun streaked the east while there were still stars in the west. Batt blew up the fire. Three dragons had strolled down to the pavement, so I rode down and ran them back. We ate with grunts and silences.

This close to the sea morning was damp. Beyond Branning, boats floated like papers towards the islands. To My Mount then, and the jerky, gentle trail down. Hisses left and right as we prodded them, but soon they were stomping and pawing in easy convergence.

Spider saw them first. "Up ahead. Who are they?"

People were running along the road; behind them, people walked. The road lights, tuned to an earlier month and longer night, went out.

Loosely curious, I rode to the head of the herd. "They're singing," I called back.

Spider looked uncomfortable. "You can hear the music?"

I nodded.

His head was still; the rest of his body swayed under his face. He switched his whip handle from hand to hand to hand; it was a quiet, beautiful way to be nervous, I thought. I played the melody for him because the sound hadn't reached us yet.

"They're singing together?"

"Yes," I told him. "They're chanting."

"Green-eye," Spider called. "Stay by me."

I put down my blade. "Is there anything wrong?"

"Maybe," Spider said. "That's the family anthem of Green-eye's line. They know he's here."

I looked questioningly.

"We wanted to get him back to Branning quietly." He flapped his dragon on the gills. "I just wonder how they found out he was coming in this morning."

I looked at Green-eye. Green-eye didn't look at me. He was watching the people along the road. I couldn't think of anything else to do, so I started to play. I didn't want to tell Spider about the man in the dog cart last night.

The voices reached us.

At which point I decided I better tell him anyway. He didn't say anything.

Suddenly Green-eye urged his dragon ahead. Spider tried

to restrain him. But he slipped beneath one hand after the other. Worry perched on his amber eyebrows. Green-eye's mount stomped ahead.

"You don't think he should go to them?" I asked.

"He knows what he's doing." The people were thick on the road. "I hope."

I watched them come, remembering Pistol. His terror must have spread over nighttime Branning like harbor oil. Dragons herded down the road; people herded up.

"What will happen?"

"They'll praise him," Spider said, "now. Later, who knows?"

"To me," I said. "I mean what's going to happen to me."

He was surprised.

"I've got to find Friza. Nothing changes. I've got to destroy the Kid. It's still the same."

I recalled the look on Pistol's face when he'd fled the Kid. Spider's face was shocked at the recognition—twisted under the same fear. But there was so much more in the face: strength rode the same muscles as terror. Yes, Spider was a large man.

"I don't care about Green-eye, or anyone else." My words were carapaced with belligerence. "I'm going down to get Friza; and I'm going to come up with her again."

"You—" he began. Then his width accepted me. "I wish you good luck." He looked again after Green-eye, swaying ahead of us towards the crowds. So much of him rode ahead with the boy. I didn't realize how much of him lingered with me. "You've done your job, then, Lobey. When we turn the herd in, you'll be paid—" He stopped. Some other thought. "Come to my house for your pay."

"Your house?"

"Yes. My home in Branning-at-sea." He coiled his whip and kneed his dragon.

We passed another signboard. The white-haired woman with the cool lips and warm eyes looked moodily at me as I rode by.

THE DOVE SAYS, "WHY HAVE NINETY-NINE WHEN NINE *THOU-SAND* ARE THERE?"

I turned away from her mocking and wondered how many people swarmed up through the morning. They lined the road. As they recognized the young herder, their song crumbled into cheering. We entered the crowd.

A jungle is a myriad of individual trees, vines, bushes; passing through, you see it, however, as one green mass. Perceiving a crowd works the same way: first the single face here (the old woman twisting her green shawl), there (the blinking boy smiling over a missing tooth) and following (three gaping girls protecting one another with their shoulders). Then the swarms of elbows and ears, tongues scraping words from the floor of the mouth and flinging them out "—move!" "Ouch! Get your—" "—I can't see" "Where is he? Is that him—" "No!" "Yes—" while the backs of the dragons undulated through the clumps of heads. They cheered. They waved their fists in the air before the gate. My job is over, I thought. People jostled My Mount. "Is that him? Is that—" The dragons were unhappy. Only Spider's calming kept them peacefully heading forward. We crowded through the gate at Branning-at-sea. At which point a lot of things happened.

I don't understand all of them. In the first few hours a lot were things that would happen to anybody who had never seen more than fifty people together at once thrust into alleys, avenues, and squares that trafficked thousands. The dragon herd left me (or I left it) to stumble about with my mouth open and my head up. People kept bumping into me and telling me to "Watch it!" which is exactly what I was trying to do; only I was trying to watch it all at the same time. Which would be difficult even if it kept still. While I watched one part, another would sneak up behind me and nearly run me down. Here's fragmenting for you:

The million's music melded to a hymn like when your ears ring and you're trying to sleep. In a village you see a face and you know it—its mother, its father, its work, how it curses, laughs, lingers on one expression, avoids another. Here one face yawns, another bulges with food; one scarred, one longing with what could be love, one screaming: each among a thousand, none seen more than once. You start to arrange the furniture in your head to find place for these faces, someplace to dump all these quarter emotions. When you go through the gate at Branning-at-sea and leave the country, you retreat to the country for your vocabulary to describe it: rivers of men and torrents of women, storms of voices, rains of fingers, and jungles of arms. But it's not fair to Branning. It's not fair to country either.

I stalked the streets of Branning-at-sea, dangling my unplayable knife, gawking at the five-story buildings till I saw the buildings with twenty-five stories. Gawked at them till I saw a building with so many stories I couldn't count, because halfway up (around ninety) I kept losing myself while people jostled me.

There were a few beautiful streets where trees rubbed their leaves over the walls. There were many filthy ones where garbage banked the sidewalk, where the houses were boxes pushed together, without room for movement of air or people. The people stayed, the air stayed; both grew foul.

On the walls were flayed posters of the Dove. Here there were others also. I passed some kids elbowing each other around one such poster that wrinkled over a fence. I squeezed among them to see what they looked at.

Two women gazed idiotically from swirling colors. The caption: "THESE TWO IDENTICAL TWINS ARE NOT THE SAME."

The youngsters giggled and shoved another. Obviously I missed something about the sign. I turned to one boy. "I don't get it."

"Huh?" He had freckles and a prosthetic arm. He scratched his head with plastic fingers. "What do you mean?"

"What's so funny about that picture?"

First disbelief: then he grinned. "If they're not the same," he blurted, *"they're different!"* They all laughed. Their laughter was filigreed with the snicker that lets you know when laughter's rotten.

I pushed away from them. I searched for music; heard none. After the listening stops, after the searching—when these sidewalks and multitudes will not bear your questions any more: that's what lonely is, Friza. Clutching my knife, I made my headlong way through evening, isolated as if I had been lost in a City.

The shingled tones of Kodaly's cello sonata. I swung around on my heels. The flags were clean and unbroken. There were trees on the corner. The buildings slanted high behind brass gates. The music unraveled in my head. Blinking, I looked from gate to gate. I chose. Faltering, I walked up the short marble steps and struck my machete hilt on the bars.

The clang leaped down the street. The sound scared me, but I struck again.

Behind the gate the brass studded door swung in. Then there was a click in the lock and the gate itself rattled loose. Cautiously, I started the walk that led to the open door. I squinted in the shadow at the doorway, then went inside, blind from the sun and alone with the music.

My eyes accustomed to the dimmer light: far ahead was a window. High in dark stone, a dragon twisted through lead tesselations.

"Lobey?"

But I have *this* against thee, that thou didst leave thy first love.

The Revelation of John, chapter 2, verse 4

My trouble is, such a subject cannot be seriously looked at without intensifying itself towards a center which is beyond what I, or anyone else, is capable of writing of . . . Trying to write it in terms of moral problems alone is more than I can possibly do. My main hope is to state the central subject and my ignorance from the start.

James Agee, "Letter to Father Flye"

Where is this country? How does one get there? If one is born lover with an innate philosophic bent, one will get there.

Plotinus, *The Intelligence, the Idea, and Being*

Spider looked up from the desk where he'd been reading. "I thought that would be you."

In shadow behind him I saw the books. La Dire had owned some hundred. But the shelves behind him went from floor to ceiling.

"I want . . . my money." My eyes came back to the desk.

"Sit down," Spider said. "I want to talk to you."

"About what?" I asked. Our voices echoed. The music was nearly silent. "I have to be on my way to get Friza, to find Kid Death."

Spider nodded. "That's why I suggest you sit down." He pressed a button, and dust motes in the air defined a long cone of light that dropped to an onyx stool. I sat slowly, holding my blade. As he had once shifted the handle of his dragon whip from hand to hand, now he played with the bleached, fragile skull of some rodent: "What do you know about mythology, Lobey?"

"Only the stories that La Dire, one of the elders of my village, used to tell me. She told all the young people stories, some of them many times. And we told them to each other till they sank into memory. But then there were other children for her to tell."

"Again, what do you know about mythology?—I'm not asking you what myths you know, nor even where they came from, but why we have them, what we use them for."

"I . . . don't know," I said. "When I left my village La Dire told me the myth of Orpheus."

Spider held up the skull and leaned forward. "Why?"

"I don't . . ." Then I thought. "To guide me?"

I could offer nothing else. Spider asked, "Was La Dire different?"

"She was—" The prurience that had riddled the laughter of the young people gaping at the poster came back to me; I did not understand it, still I felt the rims of my ear grow hot. I remembered the way Easy, Little Jon, and Lo Hawk had tried to brake my brooding over Friza; and how La Dire had tried, her attempt like theirs—yet different. "Yes," I confessed, "she was."

Spider nodded and rapped his rough knuckles on the desk. "Do you understand difference, Lobey?"

"I live in a different world, where many have it and many do not. I just discovered it in myself weeks ago. I know the world moves towards it with every pulse of the great rock and the great roll. But I don't understand it."

Through the eagerness on his drawn face Spider smiled. "In that you're like the rest of us. All any of us knows is what it is not."

"What isn't it?" I asked.

"It isn't telepathy; it's not telekinesis—though both are chance phenomena that increase as difference increases.

Lobey, Earth, the world, fifth planet from the sun—the species that stands on two legs and roams this thin wet crust: it's changing, Lobey. It's not the same. Some people walk under the sun and accept that change, others close their eyes, clap their hands to their ears, and deny the world with their tongues. Most snicker, giggle, jeer, and point when they think no one else is looking—that's how the humans acted throughout their history. We have taken over their abandoned world, and something new is happening to the fragments, something we can't even define with mankind's left-over vocabulary. You must take its importance exactly as that: it is indefinable; you are involved in it; it is wonderful, fearful, deep, ineffable to your explanations, opaque to your efforts to see through it; yet it demands you take journeys, defines your stopping and starting points, can propel you with love and hate, even to seek death for Kid Death—"

"—or make me make music," I finished for him. "What are you talking about, Spider?"

"If I could tell you, or you could understand from my inferences, Lobey, it would lose all value. Wars and chaoses and paradoxes ago, two mathematicians between them ended an age and began another for our hosts, our ghosts called Man. One was Einstein, who with his Theory of Relativity defined the limits of man's perception by expressing mathematically just how far the condition of the observer influences the thing he perceives."

"I'm familiar with it," I said.

"The other was Gödel, a contemporary of Einstein, who was the first to bring back a mathematically precise statement about the vaster realm beyond the limits Einstein had defined: *In any closed mathematical system*—you may read 'the real world with its immutable laws of logic'—*there are an infinite number of true theorems*—you may read 'perceivable, measurable phenomena'—*which, though contained in the original system, can not be deduced from it*—read 'proven with ordinary or extraordinary logic.' Which is to say, there are more things in heaven and Earth than are dreamed of in your philosophy, Lo Lobey-o. There are an infinite number of true things in the world with no way of ascertaining their truth. Einstein defined the extent of the rational. Gödel stuck a pin into the irrational and fixed it to the wall of the universe so that it held still long enough for people to know it was there. And the world and humanity began to change. And from the other side of the universe, we were drawn slowly here. The visible effects of Einstein's theory leaped up on a convex curve, its productions huge in the first century after its discovery, then leveling off. The productions of Gödel's law crept up on a concave curve, microscopic at first, then leaping to equal the Einsteinian curve, cross it, outstrip it. At the point of intersection, humanity was able to reach the limits of the known universe with ships and projection forces that are still available to anyone who wants to use them—"

"Lo Hawk," I said. "Lo Hawk went on a journey to the other worlds—"

"—and when the line of Gödel's law eagled over Einstein's, its shadow fell on a deserted Earth. The humans had gone somewhere else, to no world in this continuum. We came, took their bodies, their souls—both husks abandoned here for any wanderer's taking. The Cities, once bustling centers of interstellar commerce, were crumbled to the sands you see today. And they were once greater than Branning-at-sea."

I thought a moment. "That must have taken a long time," I said slowly.

"It has," Spider said. "The City we crossed is perhaps thirty thousand years old. The sun has captured two more planets since the Old People began here."

"And the source-cave?" I suddenly asked. "What was the source-cave?"

"Didn't you ever ask your elders?"

"Never thought to," I said.

"It's a net of caves that wanders beneath most of the planet, and the lower levels contain the source of the radiation by which the villages, when their populations become too stagnant, can set up a controlled random jumbling of genes and chromosomes. Though we have not used them for almost a thousand years, the radiation is still there. As we, templated on man, become more complicated creatures, the harder it is for us to remain perfect: there is more variation among the normals and the kages fill with rejects. And here you are, now, Lobey."

"What does this all have to do with mythology?" I was weary of his monologue.

"Recall my first question."

"What do I know of mythology?"

"And I want a Gödelian, not an Einsteinian answer. I don't want to know what's inside the myths, nor how they clang and set one another ringing, their glittering focuses, their limits and genesis. I want their shape, their texture, how they feel when you brush by them on a dark road, when you see them receding into the fog, their weight as they leap your shoulder from behind; I want to know how you take to the idea of carrying three when you already bear two. Who are you, Lobey?"

"I'm . . . Lobey?" I asked. "La Dire once called me Ringo and Orpheus."

Spider's chin rose. His fingers, caging the bone face, came together. "Yes, I thought so. Do you know who I am?"

"No."

"I'm Green-eye's Iscariot. I'm Kid Death's Pat Garrett. I'm Judge Minos at the gate, whom you must charm with your music before you can even go on to petition the Kid. I'm every traitor you've ever imagined. And I'm a baron of dragons, trying to support two wives and ten children."

"You're a big man, Spider."

He nodded. "What do you know of mythology?"

"Now that's the third time you've asked me." I picked up my blade. From the grinding love that wanted to serenade his silences—the music had all stopped—I leaned the blade against my teeth.

"Bite through the shells of my meanings, Lobey. I know so much more than you. The guilty have the relief of knowledge."

He held the skull over the table. I thought he was offering it to me. "I know where you can find Friza. I can let you through the gate. Though Kid Death may kill me, I want you to know that. He is younger, crueler, and much stronger. Do you want to go on?"

I dropped my blade. "It's fixed!" I said. "I'll fail! La Dire said Orpheus failed. You're trying to tell me that those stories tell us just what is going to happen. You've been telling me we're so much older than we think we are; this is all schematic for a reality I can't change! You're telling me right now that I've failed as soon as I start."

"Do you believe that?"

"That's what you've said."

"As we are able to retain more and more of our past, it takes us longer and longer to become old; Lobey, everything changes. The labyrinth today does not follow the same path it did at Knossos fifty thousand years ago. You may be Orpheus; you may be someone else, who dares death and succeeds. Green-eye may go to the tree this evening, hang there, rot, and never come down. The world is not the same. That's what I've been trying to tell you. It's different."

"But—"

"There's just as much suspense today as there was when the first singer woke from his song to discover the worth of the concomitant sacrifice. You don't know, Lobey. This all may be a false note, at best a passing dissonance in the harmonies of the great rock and the great roll."

I thought for a while. Then I said, "I want to run away."

Spider nodded. "Some mason set the double-headed labrys on the stones at Pheistos. You carry a two-edge knife that sings. One wonders if Theseus built the maze as he wandered through it."

"I don't think so," I said, defensive and dry. "The stories give you a law to follow—"

"—that you can either break or obey.

"They set you a goal—"

"—and you can either fail that goal, succeed, or surpass it."

"Why?" I demanded. "Why can't you just ignore the old stories? I'll go on plumb the sea, find the Kid without your help. I can ignore those tales!"

"You're living in the real world now," Spider said sadly. "It's come from something. It's going to something. Myths always lie in the most difficult places to ignore. They confound all family love and hate. You shy at them on entering or exiting any endeavor." He put the skull on the table. "Do you know why the Kid needs you as much as he needs Green-eye?"

I shook my head.

"I do."

"The Kid needs me?"

"Why do you think you're here?"

"Is the reason . . . different?"

"Primarily. Sit back and listen." Spider himself leaned back in his chair. I stayed where I was. "The Kid can change anything in the range of his intelligence. He can make a rock into a tree, a mouse into a handful of moss. But he cannot create something from nothing. He cannot take this skull and leave a vacuum. Green-eye can. And that is why the Kid needs Green-eye."

I remembered the encounter on the mountain where the malicious redhead had tried to tempt the depthless vision of the herder-prince.

"The other thing he needs is music, Lobey."

"Music?"

"This is why he is chasing you—or making you chase him. He needs order. He needs patterning, relation, the knowledge that comes when six notes predict a seventh, when three notes beat against one another and define a mode, a melody defines a scale. Music is the pure language of temporal and co-temporal relation. He knows nothing of this, Lobey. Kid Death can control, but he cannot create, which is why he needs Green-eye. He can control, but he cannot order. And that is why he needs you."

"But how—?"

"Not in any way your village vocabulary or my urban refinement can state. Differently, Lobey. Things passing in a world of difference have their surrealistic corollaries in the present. Green-eye creates, but it is an oblique side effect of something else. You receive and conceive music; again only an oblique characteristic of who you are—"

"*Who* am I?"

"You're . . . something else."

My question had contained a demand. His answer held a chuckle.

"But he needs you both," Spider went on. "What are you going to give him?"

"My knife in his belly till blood floods the holes and leaks out the mouthpiece. I'll chase the sea-floor till we both fall on sand. I—" My mouth opened; I suddenly sucked in dark air so hard it hurt my chest. "I'm afraid," I whispered. "Spider, I'm afraid."

"Why?"

I looked at him behind the evenly blinking lids of his black eyes. "Because I didn't realize I'm alone in this." I slid my hands together on the hilt. "If I'm to get Friza, I have to go alone—not with her love, but without it. You're not on my side." I felt my voice roughen, not with fear. It was the sadness that starts in the back of the throat and makes you cough before you start crying. "If I reach Friza, I don't know what I'll have, even if I get her."

Spider waited for my crying. I wouldn't give him the satisfaction. So after a while he said, "Then I guess I can let you through, if you really know that."

I looked up.

He nodded to my silent question.

"There's someone you must go to see. Here." He stood up. In his other hand was a small sack. He shook it. Inside coins clinked. He flung the sack towards me. I caught it.

"Who?"

"The Dove."

"The one whose pictures I've seen? But who—"

"Who is the Dove?" asked Spider. "The Dove is Helen of

Troy, Starr Anthim, Mario Montez, Jean Harlow." He waited. "And you?" I asked. "You're Judas and Minos and Pat Garrett? Who are you to her?"

His snort was contemptuous and amused. "If the Dove is Jean Harlow I'm Paul Burn."

"But why—?"

"Come on, Lobey. Get going."

"I'm going," I said. "I'm going." I was confused. For much the same reasons you are. Though not *exactly* the same. As I walked to the door I kept glancing back at Spider. Suddenly he tossed the skull gently. It passed me, hovered a moment, then smashed on the stones; and Spider laughed. It was a friendly laugh, without the malicious flickering of fish scales and flies' wings that dazzled the laughter of the Kid. But it nearly scared me to death. I ran out of the door. For one step bone fragments chewed at my instep. The door slammed behind me. The sun slapped my face.

Leave Crete and come to this holy temple.

Sappho, "Fragment"

This morning I took refuge from the thin rain in a tea-house with the dock workers. Yellow clouds moiled outside above the Bosphorus. Found one man who spoke French, two others who spoke Greek. We talked of voyages and warmed our fingers on glasses of tea. Between the four of us we had girdled the globe. The radio over the stove alternated repetitive Turkish modulations with Aznavour and the Beatles. Lobey starts the last leg of his journey. I cannot follow him here. When the rain stopped, I walked through the waterfront fish market where the silver fish had their gills pulled out and looped over their jaws so that each head was crowned with a bloody flower. A street of wooden houses wound up the hill into the city. A fire had recently raged here. Few houses had actually burned down, but high slabs of glittering carbon leaned over the cobbles where the children played with an orange peel in the mud. I watched some others chase a redheaded boy. His face was wet; he tripped in the mud, then fled before me. The backs had been trod down on his shoes. Perhaps on rewriting I shall change Kid Death's hair from black to red. Followed the wall of Topkapi palace, kicking away wet leaves from the pavement. I stopped in the Sultanahmet Jammi. The blue designs rose on the dome above me. It was restful. In a week another birthday, and I can start the meticulous process of overlaying another filigree across the novel's palimpsest. The stones were cold under my bare feet. The designs keep going, taking your eyes up and out of yourself. Outside I put on my boots and started across the courtyard. In the second story of the old teahouse across the park I sat in a corner away from the stove and tried to wrestle my characters towards their endings. Soon I shall start again. Endings to be useful must be inconclusive.

Writer's Journal, Istanbul, March 1966

What are your qualifications? Dare you dwell in the East where we dwell? Are you afraid of the sun? When you hear the new violet sucking her way among the clods, shall you be resolute?

Emily Dickinson, "Letter to K. S. Turner"

The Pearl surprised me. A million people is too many to sort an individual from a slum. But the established classes are all the more centralized. There in the furious evening I saw the sign down the street. I looked in my purse. But Spider would have given me enough.

Black doors broke under a crimson sunburst. I went up the stairs beneath the orange lights. There was perfume. There was noise. I held my sword tight. Tack-heads had worn away the nap of the carpet with the tugging of how many feet. Someone had painted a *trompe l'oeil* still life on the left wall: fruit, feathers, and surveying instruments on crumpled leather. Voices, yes. Still, at the place where the auditory nerve connects to the brain and sound becomes music, there was silence.

"Lo?" inquired the dog at the head of the steps.

I was baffled. "Lo Lobey," I told his cold face, and grinned at it. It stayed cold.

And on the balcony across the crowded room where her party was, she stood up, leaned over the railing, called, "Who are you?" with contralto laughter spilling her words.

She was pretty. She wore silver, a sheath V'd deeply between small breasts. Her mouth seemed used to emotions, mostly laughter I guessed. Her hair was riotous and bright as

Little Jon's. The person she was calling to was me. "Um-hm. You, silly. Who are you?"

It had slipped my mind that when somebody speaks to you, you answer. The dog coughed, then announced. "Eh . . . Lo Lobey is here." At which point everyone in the room silenced. With the silence I learned how noisy it had been. Glasses, whispers, laughter, talk, feet on the floor, chair legs squeaking after them: I wished it would start again. In a doorway on the side of the room where two serpents twined over the transom, I saw the fat, familiar figure of the hunchback Pistol. He was obviously coming from somewhere to see what was wrong; he saw me, closed his eyes, took a breath, and leaned on the door jamb.

Then the Dove said, "Well, it's about time, Lo Lobey. I thought you'd never get here. Pistol, bring a chair."

I was surprised. Pistol was astounded. But after he got his mouth closed, he got the chair. With drawn machete I stalked the Dove among the tables, the flowers, the candles and cut goblets; the men with gold chained dogs crouching at their sandals; the women with jeweled eyelids, their breasts propped in cages of brass mesh or silver wire. They all turned to watch me as I went.

I mounted the stairway to the Dove's balcony. One hip against the railing, she held out her hand to me. "You're Spider's friend," she beamed. She made you feel very good when she talked. "Pistol"—she twisted around; wrinkles of light slid over her dress—"put the seat before mine." He did and we sat on the brocade cushions.

With the Dove in front of me it was a little difficult to look at anyone else. She leaned towards me, breathing. I guess that's what she was doing. "We're supposed to talk. What do you want to talk about?"

Breathing is a fascinating thing to watch in a woman. "Eh . . . ah . . . well . . ." I pulled my attention forcefully back to her face. "Are nine thousand really that much better than ninety-nine?" (You think I knew what I was talking about?) She began to laugh without making any sound. Which is even more fascinating.

"Ah!" she responded, "you must try it and find out."

At which point everybody started talking again. The Dove still watched me. "What do you do?" I asked. "Spider says you're supposed to help me find Friza."

"I don't know who Friza is."

"She was—" The Dove was breathing again. "—beautiful too."

Her face passed down to deeper emotion. "Yes," she said.

"I don't think we can talk about it here." I glanced at Pistol, who was still hovering. "The problem isn't exactly the same as you might think."

She raised a darkened eyebrow.

"It's a bit . . ."

"Oh," she said, and her chin went up.

"But you?" I said. "What do you do? Who are you?"

Her eyebrow arch grew more acute. "Are you serious?" I nodded.

In confusion she looked to the people around her. When no one offered to explain for her, she looked back at me. Her lips opened, touched; her lashes dipped and leaped. "They say I'm the thing that allows them all to go on loving."

"How?" I asked.

Someone beside her said, "He really doesn't know?"

From the other side: "Doesn't he know about keeping confusion in the trails fertile?"

She placed a finger perpendicular to her lips. They quieted at the sound of her sigh. "I'll have to tell him. Lobey—this is your . . . name."

"Spider told me to talk to you . . ." I offered. I wanted to fix myself by informative hooks to her world.

Her smile cut guys. "You try to make things too simple. Spider. The great Lord Lo Spider? The traitor, the false friend, the one who has already signed Green-eye's death decree. Don't concern yourself with that doomed man. Look to yourself, Lobey. What do you want to know—"

"Death decree—"

She touched my cheek. "Be selfish. What do you want?"

122 ❍ SAMUEL R. DELANY

"Friza!" I half stood from my seat.

She sat back. "Now I'll ask you a question, having not answered yours. Who is Friza?"

"She . . ." Then I said, "She was almost as beautiful as you."

Her chin came down. Light, light eyes darkened and came down too. "Yes." That word came with the sound of only the breath I had been watching, without voice. So much questioning in her face now made her remembered expression caustic.

"I . . ." The wrong word. "She . . ." A fist started to beat my ribs. Then it stopped, opened, reached up into my head, and scratched down the inside of my face: forehead and cheeks burned. My eyes stung.

She caught her breath. "I see."

"No you don't," I got out. "You don't."

They were watching again. She glanced right, left, bit her lip as she looked back. "You and I are . . . well, not quite the same."

"Huh? . . . oh. But—Dove—"

"Yes, Lobey?"

"Where am I? I've come from a village, from the wilds of nowhere, through dragons and flowers. I've thrown my Lo, searching out my dead girl, hunting a naked cowboy mean as Spider's whip. And somewhere a dirty, one-eyed prince is going to . . . die while I go on. Where am I, Dove?"

"This close to an old place called Hell." She spoke quickly. "You can enter it through death or song. But you may need some help to find your way out."

"I look for my dark girl and find you silver."

She stood, and blades of light struck at me from her dress. Her smooth hand swung by her hip. I grabbed it with my rough one. "Come," she said.

I came.

As we descended from the balcony she leaned on my arm. "We are going to walk once around the room. I suppose you have the choice either of listening, or watching. I doubt if you can do both. I couldn't, but try." As we started to circuit the room, I beat my shin with the flat of my sword.

"We are worn out with trying to be human, Lobey. To survive even a dozen more generations we must keep the genes mixing, mixing, mixing."

An old man leaned his belly on the edge of his table, gaping at the girl across from him. She licked the corner of her mouth, her eyes wondrous and blue and beautiful. Her cheekbones mocked him.

"You can't force people to have children with many people. But we can make the idea as attractive"—she dropped her eyes—"as possible."

At the next table the woman's face was too loose for the framing bone beneath. But she laughed. Her hand wrinkled over the smooth fingers of the young man across from her. She gazed enviously from lined eyes at his quick lids, dark as olives when he blinked, his hair shinier than hers, wild where hers was coiffed in high lacquer.

"Who am I, Lobey?" she suggested—rather than asked—rhetorically. "I'm the key image in an advertising campaign. I'm the good/bad wild thing whom everybody wants, wants to be like—who prefers ninety-nine instead of one. I'm the one whom men search out from seeding to seeding. I'm the one whom all the women style their hair after, raise and lower their hems and necklines as mine rise and lower. The world steals my witticisms, my gestures, even my mistakes, to try out on each new lover."

The couple at the next table had probably forgotten most of what it was like to be forty. They looked happy, wealthy, and content. I was envious.

"There was a time," the Dove went on, pressing the back of my hand with her forefinger, "when orgies and artificial insemination did the trick. But we still have a jelling attitude to melt. So, that's what I do. Which leaves you, I gather, with another question."

The youngsters across from us clutched each other's hands and giggled. Once I thought that twenty-one was the responsible age; it had to be, it was so far away. Those kids could do anything and were just learning how, and were hurt and astounded and deliriously happy at once with the prospects.

"The answer"—and I looked back at the Dove—"lies with the particular talent I have that facilitates my job."

The finger that had pressed my hand now touched my lips. She pouted for silence. With her other hand she lifted my sword. "Play, Lobey?"

"For you?"

She swept her hand around the room. "For them." She turned to the people. "Everybody! I want you to be quiet. I want you to hear. You must be still—"

They stilled.

"—and listen."

They listened. Many leaned their elbows on the table. The Dove turned to me and nodded. I looked at my machete.

Across the room Pistol was holding his head. I smiled at him. Then I sat down on the edge of an empty table, toed the holes, fingered them.

I blew a note. I looked at the people. I blew another one. I laughed after that one.

The youngsters laughed too.

I blew two notes, down, then shrill.

I started to clap my hands, a hard, slow rhythm. I made the melody with feet alone. The kids thought that was pretty funny too. I rocked on the table edge, closed my eyes, and clapped and played. In the back somebody began to clap with me. I grinned into the flute (difficult) and the sound brightened. I remembered the music I'd got from Spider. So I tried something I'd never done before. I let one melody go on without my playing it, and played another instead. Tones tugged each other into harmony as they swooped from clap to clap. I let those two continue and threaded a third above them. I pushed the music into a body swayer, a food shaker, till fingers upon the tablecloth pounced on the pattern. I played, looking hard at them, weighing the weight of music in them, and when there was enough, I danced. Movements repeated themselves; making dances is the opposite of taking them. I danced on the table. Hard. I whipped them with music. Sound peeled from sound. Chords fell open like sated flowers. People called out. I shrilled my rhythms at them down the hollow knife, gouged notes down their spines the way you pith a frog. They shook in their seats. I put into the music a fourth line, dissonant to lots and lots of others. Three people had started dancing with me. I made the music make them. Rhythm buoyed their jerking. The old man was shaking his shoulders at the blue-eyed girl. Clap. The youngsters shook shoulder—Clap—to shoulder. The older couple held hands very tightly. Clap. Sound banked behind— Clap—itself. Silence a moment. Clap. Then loosed through the room, like dragons in the gorse, wild, they moaned together, beat their thighs and bellies to four melodies.

On the raised dais, where the Dove's table had been, somebody opened the wide windows. The wind on my sweaty back made me cough. The cough growled in the flute. A breeze in a closed room lets you know how hot it is. The dancers moved to the balcony. I followed them. The tiles were red and blue. The gold evening streamed with blue wounds. One or two dancers rested on the railing. My sword fell from my lips as I gazed around the—

It caught me across the eyes. The silver dress rippled in the wind. But it wasn't the Dove. She raised dark knuckles to her brown cheek, her full mouth parting in a sigh. She blinked, brushed her hand across her hair, searching through the dancers. One and another of them hid her a moment, stepped away.

Dark Friza—

Friza returned and turning among the dancers—

Beautiful and longed for Friza, found—

Once I was so hungry that when I ate I was frightened. The same fear now. Only more. The music played itself. The blade hung in my hand. Once Friza had thrown a pebble—

I began to run the maze of dancers.

She saw me. I caught her shoulders; she clutched me, cheek on my neck, breast on my breast, her arms hard across my back. Her name swam in my head. I know I hurt her. Her fists on my back hurt me. My eyes were wide and tearing. I wanted to be open to everything about her. Nothing shook in her. I held all her slim strength. My arms tightened, relaxed, tightened again.

Across the park below was a single tree, wintered by the insane sun. Roped from the crotch, one arm to each fork, head so far forward the neck had to be broken, dangled Greeneye. Blood from a rope cut glittered along his arm.

She twisted in my arms, looked at me, at what I looked at. Quickly she put her hands over my eyes. Alone behind her dark fingers, I recognized the music. Polyphonized and danced by strangers, it was the mourning song of the girl who shielded my eyes now, played for the garroted prince.

Under the music, a voice whispered, "Lobey, be careful." It was the Dove's voice. "Do you want to look that closely?"

The fingers stayed over my face.

"I can look down your head like a hall. You died, Lobey. Somewhere in the rocks and rain, you died. Do you want to look at that closely—"

"I'm no ghost!"

"Oh, you're real, Lobey! But perhaps—"

I twisted my head again, but darkness followed.

"Do you want to know about the Kid?"

"I want to know anything that'll help me kill him."

"Then listen. Kid Death can bring back to life only the ones he himself takes from it. He can only keep the belly buttons he harvests. But do you know who brought you back from—"

"Take your hands away."

"You've got a choice to make, Lobey, quick!" the Dove whispered. "Do you want to see what's in front of you? Or do you want to see only what you saw before?"

"Your hands. I can't see anything with your hands in front of my . . ." I stopped, horrified at what I had just said.

"I'm very talented, Lobey, in what I do." Light seeped in, as gently the pressure released. "I've had to perfect that talent

to survive. You can't ignore the laws of the world you've cho-
sen—"

I took the wrists and pulled the hands down. The Dove's
hands resisted just a moment, then fell. Green-eye was still
roped to the tree below me.

I grabbed the Dove's arms. "Where *is* she?" I looked about
the terrace. I shook her and she pulled back against the rail.

"I become the thing you love, Lobey. That's part of my talent. That's how I can be the Dove."

I shook my head. "But you—"

She rubbed her shoulder. Her hand slid under the silver
cloth. It shifted with her fingers.

"And they—" I gestured towards the dancers. The youngsters, still holding hands, were pointing into the park and
giggling. "They call you La Dove."

She cocked her head, brushing back silver hair. "No,
Lobey." She shook her head. "Who told you that, Lobey?
Who told you that? I'm Le Dove."

I got chills. The Dove extended a slim hand. "Didn't you
know? Lobey, you mean you didn't—"

I backed away, raising my sword.

"Lobey, we're not human! We live on their planet, because
they destroyed it. We've tried to take their form, their memories, their myths. But they don't fit. It's illusion, Lobey. So
much of it. He brought you back: Green-eye. He's the one
who could have brought back, *really* brought back your
Friza."

"Green-eye . . . ?"

"But we're just not the same as they were, Lobey. We're—"

I turned and ran from the balcony.

Inside, I overturned a table, whirled at the barking dog.
"Lo Lobey!" He sat on the dais where the Dove's party had
been. "Come. Have you been enjoying the floor show here at
the Pearl?"

Before I could say anything, he nosed a switch in the wall.

The floor began to rotate. Through my hysteria I realized
what was happening. The floor was two panes of polarized

plastic, one above the other. The top one turned; the lower one was still. As they reached transparency, I saw figures moving below in the crevices of the stone, down below the chair and table legs.

"The Pearl is built over one of the corridors for the kage at Branning-at-sea. Look: they weave there among the crags, that one falling, that other clinging to the wall, chewing his tongue and drooling blood. We have no kage-keeper here. The old computer system the humans used for Psychic Harmony and Entangled Deranged Response Associations takes care of their illusions. Down there is a whole hell full of gratified desire—"

I flung myself on the floor, pressing my face against the transparency. "PHAEDRA!" I screamed. "PHAEDRA, where is she?"

"Hi, baby!" Lights glittered below me from the shadow. A couple with many too many arms stood in a quiet embrace beneath the flickering machine.

"PHAEDRA—"

"It's still the wrong maze, baby. You can find another illusion down here. She'll follow you all the way to the door, but when you turn around to make sure she's there, you'll see through it all again, and you'll leave alone. Why even bother to go through with it?" The voice was thinned through the plastic floor. "Mother is in charge of everything down here. Don't come playing your bloody knife around me. You've got to try and get her back some other way. You're a bunch of psychic manifestations, multisexed and incorporeal, and you—you're all trying to put on the limiting mask of humanity. Turn again, Lobey. Seek somewhere outside the frame of the mirror—"

"Where—"

"Have you begged at the tree?"

Below me the lost drooled and lurched and jabbered in the depths of the kage beneath PHAEDRA's flickering. I pushed away. The dog barked as I reached the door.

I missed a stair and grabbed the banister four steps down.

The building hurled me into the park. I caught my balance. Around the plaza metal towers roared with spectators dancing on the terraces, singing from crowded windows.

I stood before the tree and played to him, pleading. I hung chords on a run of sevenths that begged his resolution. I began humbly, and the song emptied me, till there was only the pit. I plunged. There was rage. It was mine, so I gave him that. There was love. That shrilled beneath the singing in the windows.

Where his forearm had been lashed to the branch, the bone had broken. His hand sagged away from the bark and—

—and nothing. I shrieked, as outrage broke. With the hilt in both hands, I plunged the point in his thigh, sank it to the wood. I screamed again and wrenched away, quivering.

In pity for man's darkening thought
He walked that room and issued thence
In Galilean turbulence;
The Babylonian starlight brought
a fabulous, formless darkness in.
William Butler Yeats, "Song from a Play"

I have heard that you will give 1000 dollars for my body
which as I understand it, means as a witness . . . if it was
so as I could appear in court, I would give the desired information, but I have indictments against me for things
that happened in the Lincoln County War, and am afraid
to give myself up because my enemies would kill me.
William H. Bonney (Billy the Kid),
"Letter to Lt.-Gov. Lew Wallace"

I seek with garlands to redress that wrong.
Andrew Marvell, "The Coronet"

The sea broke. Morning ran over the water. I walked along
the beach alone. There were a lot of shells around. I kept on
thinking, just a day before we rode into Branning on dragons. Now his life and my illusions were gone. Behind me
Branning-at-sea diminished on the dawn. The point of my
machete scarred the sand again and again as I walked.

I was not tired. I'd walked all night. But something had
wound the ends of fatigue so tight I couldn't stop. The dawn
beach was beautiful. I climbed a dune crested with long, lisp-
ing grasses.

"Hey, Lobey."

Whatever it was unwound and shook like sprung clock-works.

"How you been?"

He was sitting on a log jammed into the moist sand at the bottom of the dune. He squinted up at me, brushed back his hair. The sun flamed the crystals on his shoulder, his arm: salt.

"I been waiting a long, long time." He scratched his knee. "How are you?"

"I don't know," I said. "Tired."

"Are you going to play?" He pointed up at my sword. "Come on down."

"I don't want to," I said.

Sand trickled from the soles of my feet. I looked down, just as a piece of dune fell away beneath me. I staggered. Fear jogged loose. I fell, and began to claw at the ground. While the Kid chuckled, I slipped down the slope. At the bottom, I whirled. The Kid, still sitting on the log, looked down at me.

"What do you want?" I whispered. "You've lost Green-eye. What do you want from me?"

The Kid rubbed his ear, smiling over many small teeth. "I need that." He pointed to my machete. "Do you think Spider would really—" He stopped. "Spider decided Green-eye, you, and me couldn't stay alive in the same world; it was too dangerous. So he signed the death decree and had Green-eye strung up while you played him out, and I cried beneath the sea where you can't see tears; is that what you believe?"

"I don't . . . I don't know."

"I believe that Green-eye lives. I don't know. I can't follow him like I can the rest of you. He could be dead." He leaned forward and bared his teeth. "But he's not."

I pushed my back against the sand.

"Give me your sword."

I pulled back my arm. Suddenly I swung forward and hacked at him. He dodged. Wood splintered.

"If you hit me," he said, "I suppose it would be unpleasant. I do bleed. But if I can tell what you're thinking, well then, attempts to get rid of me like that are really fruitless." He shrugged, smiling, reached out, and touched the blade.

My hand jumped. He took the machete, fingered the holes. "No," he sighed. "No, that doesn't do me any good." He held it out to me again. "Show me how?"

I took it from him because it was mine and I didn't like him holding it.

He scratched his right heel with his left foot, "Come on. Show me. I don't need the knife. I need the music inside. Play, Lobey." He nodded.

Terrified, I put the handle to my mouth.

"Go on."

A note quavered.

He leaned forward, gold lashes low. "Now I'm gonna take everything that's left." His fingers snared one another. He curled his toes, tearing earth.

Another note.

I began a third—

It was a sound and a motion and a feeling all at once. It was a loud *snap*: the Kid arched his back and grabbed his neck; the feeling was terror going a few degrees farther than I thought it could. Spider, from the top of the dune shouted, "Keep playing, damn it!"

I squawked through the blade.

"As long as you make music, he can't use his mind for anything else!"

The Kid was standing. The dragon whip lashed over my head. Blood lanced down his chest. He stumbled back over the driftwood, fell. I scrambled aside, managing to keep my feet under me—a trifle easier for me than most other people. I was still getting some sort of noise out of the knife.

Spider, his whip singing, came crabwise down the dune.

The Kid flipped to his belly under the lash and tried to crawl. The gills spread, redder that the coppery hair falling wetly over his neck. Spider cut his back open, then yelled at me, "Don't stop playing!"

The Kid hissed and bit the ground. He rolled to his side,

sand on his mouth and chin. "Spider . . . aw, Spider. Stop it! Don't, please . . . don—" The whip opened his cheek and he clutched his face.

"Keep playing, Lobey! Damn it, or he'll kill me!"

Overblown at the octave, my notes jabbed the morning.

"Ahhhhh . . . no, Spider-man. Don't hurt me no more!" His speech slurred on his bloody tongue. "Don't— ahhh *hhh*—it hurts. It hurts! You're supposed to be my friend, Spider!—naw, you're supposed to be my . . ." Sobs for a while. The whip cut the Kid again and again.

Spider's shoulders ran with sweat. "Okay," he said. He coiled his lash, breathing hard.

My tongue was sore, my hands numb. Spider looked from me to the Kid. "It's over," he said.

"Was it . . . necessary?" I asked.

Spider just looked at the ground.

There was a thrashing in the bush. A length of thorn coiled over the sand, dragging a blossom.

Spider started up the slope. "Come on," he said. I followed him. At the top I looked back. A bouquet clustered over the corpse's head, jostling for eyes and tongue. I followed Spider down.

At the bottom he turned to me. Then he frowned. "Snap out of it, boy. I just saved your life—that's all."

"Spider . . . ?"

"What?"

"Green-eye . . . I think I've figured something out."

"What? . . . Come on, we have to get back."

"Like the Kid; I can bring back the ones I've killed myself."

"Like in the broken land," Spider said. "You brought yourself back. You let yourself die, and you came back. Green-eye is the only one who can bring your Friza back—now."

"Green-eye," I said again. "He's dead."

Spider nodded. "You killed him. It was that last stroke of your . . ." He gestured towards my machete.

"Oh," I said. "What's going on back at Branning-at-sea?"

"Riots."

"Why?"

"They're hungry for their own future." For a moment I pictured the garden of the Kid's face. It made me ill.

"I'm going back," he said. "Are you coming?"

The sea receded and froth spiraled the sand.

I thought for a while. "Yes. But not now."

"Green-eye will"—Spider mashed something into the sand with his foot—"wait, I suppose. And the Dove too. The Dove leads them in the dance, now, and won't be so ready to forgive you for the choice you made."

"What was it?"

"Between the real and—the rest."

"Which did I choose?"

Spider pushed my shoulder, grinning. "Maybe you'll know when you get back. Where you off to?" He started to turn.

"Spider?"

He looked back.

"In my village there was a man who grew dissatisfied. So he left this world, worked for a while on the moon, on the outer planets, then on worlds that were stars and stars away. I might go there."

Spider nodded. "I did that once. It was all waiting for me when I got back."

"What's it going to be like?"

"It's not going to be what you expect." He grinned, then turned away.

"It's going to be . . . different?"

He kept walking down the sand.

As morning branded the sea, darkness fell away at the far side of the beach. I turned to follow it.

—New York, Paris, Venice,
Athens, Istanbul, London,
Sept '65–Nov '66

University Press of New England
publishes books under its own imprint and is the publisher for Brandeis University Press, Dartmouth College, Middlebury College Press, University of New Hampshire, Tufts University, and Wesleyan University Press.

About the Authors

Samuel R. Delany is best known as the author of science fiction and fantasy novels; his books have won Hugo and Nebula awards. In addition to his fiction, he has published many books of nonfiction, including semiotic studies of literature and a volume of memoirs. Delany is currently professor of comparative literature at the University of Massachusetts at Amherst.

Neil Gaiman is best known for writing the series of graphic novels that comprise *The Sandman*, published in ten volumes by DC Comics. It is the recipient of more awards internationally than any other work written for the comics medium, including the World Fantasy Award, making it the only comic to have received an award intended for prose fiction. Having recently written the saga of Beowulf as a Hollywood movie, he is currently working on a short story collection and a new, prose, novel.

Library of Congress Cataloging-in-Publication Data
Delany, Samuel R.
    The Einstein intersection / Samuel R. Delany.
       p. cm.
    ISBN 0–8195–6336–6 (pbk. : alk. paper)
    I. Title.
PS3554.E437E45   1998
813'.54—dc21   97–44598